VAGRANT

VAGRANT

USA TODAY BESTSELLING AUTHOR

GEMMA JAMES

Note To Readers

Vagrant is a new adult dark romance with disturbing themes and explicit content, including sexual scenes and violence that may offend some. Intended for mature audiences. Part four of the Condemned series.

To my family. Thanks for putting up with me.

1. I'M COMING FOR YOU

ALEX

"You must be one badass chick," Leslie the tattoo artist said. "You didn't flinch once through the whole thing."

"Pain doesn't bother me." Not the kind you could see, anyway. The scars on the inside healed much slower than the welts from a cane or the cuts from a knife.

"Looks good," she said, standing at my side in front of the mirror. Rafe's name concealed the carving of Zach's in scrawling black ink. The tattoo spanned a good portion of my belly in wispy tribal lines, butterflies in flight, and those four important letters. Having his name permanently inked on my skin made me feel close to him.

Even if he was a liar.

I love you. See you soon.

1

Six months later and those words still haunted me.

They said there were five stages of the grieving process, but I wondered who the nebulous they were. Since the day Jax returned to the safe house and told me Rafe was gone, I'd spent most of my time locked in step one of the natural progression of grieving: *denial*.

Of course he was coming back. He'd promised. Maybe Jax didn't know what he was talking about. Maybe Rafe had lost the remainder of his memory and was stranded somewhere, confused and alone. Maybe he'd made it out of Lucas' house and couldn't remember how to get back to me.

Maybe, maybe, maybe.

But Rafe wasn't coming back. Deep down, I'd known it with one glance at Jax's distraught, bloodied face.

So that brought me to step two. I was angry. Angry at Rafe for leaving me in the first place, chained to his bed with the promise of our future playing on repeat in my mind. Angry I was stuck in denial. I somehow skipped past the third stage of *bargaining* because let's face it—I was screwed. If anyone existed beyond this plane of existence, they sure as hell weren't listening to me.

Which led to step four: depression. I'd been in a perpetual state of melancholy for years, so that was nothing new. But the last stage, the holy grail of letting go and moving on...

Acceptance.

It sounded good, in theory. After attempting to put my jagged pieces back together, I wanted to accept he was gone. It was the reason I'd gotten the tattoo, my first baby step toward wiping clean what Zach had done.

"That should be the last touch up, hon." Leslie squeezed my shoulder. "Unless you want to start on something new, you're good to go."

I was about to embark on something that scared the shit out of me, and it had nothing to do with getting another tattoo. The compulsion to visit the island had trapped me in purgatory, and until I laid eyes on it, I wouldn't move forward.

I gave Leslie a sad smile, thanked her for her work, and stepped into the frigid air with my pulse thrumming a furious tempo in my veins. The drive to Dante's Pass seemed to blur by in slow motion, yet the seconds ticked by too fast. I exited the highway and rolled down Main Street, my foot tapping the brake as snow drifted to the ground. I half slid, half wheeled into a parking spot and got out, my boots sinking into the fluffy white.

The place was frozen, desolate, the streets bereft. Most people had holed up inside to escape the snow. The setting was an uncanny snapshot of the way I felt on the inside. Rafe was gone, but the space where my heart used to reside only grew bigger with each day I faced alone. Time hadn't dulled the pain, hadn't eased the betrayal of abandonment. I'd finally accepted he was gone, and that meant I had nothing left to do but *live*.

It's what he would have wanted, but living for me turned out more challenging than I imagined. My dad and Zach had always dictated my decisions, actions, behaviors. Now that I'd grasped control of my life, I felt imprisoned, out of my element and absolutely terrified.

Every breath I took, each new cautious step toward the future…Rafe's absence kept me in a constant choke hold, his metaphorical fingers clamping around my neck but not applying enough pressure to send me into blackness.

I blinked the snow from my lashes and gazed at the picturesque street with its shops and cafes. The day Rafe brought me here to tell the sheriff what Zach had done was a fuzzy memory, but I recognized this street, despite the layer of snow covering the asphalt.

A breath shuddered out. I shouldn't have come here. It was too soon, and setting foot in the place where he'd grown up wasn't going to help me move on. How could I lay eyes on that island without fissuring? But it drew me like a magnet. I needed to know if the fire had destroyed the land as much as Rafe leaving had destroyed me.

Leaving.

I couldn't bring myself to use the word death in relation to him. He didn't *feel* gone forever. I was still breathing, so he had to be alive. Didn't matter if my logic was skewed; I gripped it with both hands.

I took a final glance down the main street of Dante's Pass, committing it to memory, and returned to my Volvo. I drove onto the highway again, and the island came into view, rising out of the water with barren landscape overrun by snow. An artist could use that scene to paint a morbid picture of winter desolation. Nature might wipe away some of the destruction, but it couldn't hide it entirely.

Just like the smile I pasted on my face couldn't hide the cracks in my soul, but I wore it anyway, especially when I worked at Sanctuary, a shelter for battered women and children. Those women found it easy to confide in me because they saw themselves in the broken girl who spent more time with them than she did living. I loved working there, actually felt like I was making a difference, even if I only did the bookkeeping. I spent more hours at that place, working and volunteering, than doing anything else. I was good at helping others with their trauma and grief because I sure couldn't shake my own.

I rolled to a stop on the side of the highway and slid from the driver's seat, leaving the door open and the engine running. With a hard swallow, I stepped over the rail and tiptoed toward the edge of the river. The water's surface whispered to me from several feet below. I'd come a long way, in terms of my phobia, but my irrational fear was still an everyday struggle.

Lifting my gaze, I focused on the island with even

breaths. My hands formed two tight balls of sheer willpower—if I unfurled my fists, I wouldn't be able to stop from scratching my skin. The compulsion nearly overwhelmed me, but I drew on my breathing technique and mentally recited what my therapist often said to me.

You have the power to change your life.

No one else could do it for me, and I was fed up with mutilating my skin because I couldn't cope.

A gust of wind nipped at my exposed cheeks. I pulled my jacket tighter, nestling deep into the hood. Coming here was hard, but it was the only way I knew how to let Rafe go. I'd tried everything to find him somewhere alive. I'd badgered Jax for the truth about that morning until he'd stormed off without a word. And after hearing rumors that Rafe was involved in illegal fighting, I'd hired a private investigator, but he'd turned up dead end after dead end.

If Rafe was alive, he either didn't know who he was… or he didn't want to be found.

Eyes stinging, I shivered in my boots and slid behind the wheel again. As I left Dante's Pass, hot tears streamed down my cheeks. I was surprised I made it home in one piece, considering the wretched weather and the state of my mind.

The one bedroom house where I now lived was dinky compared to my home before they'd arrested Dad, but I paid for the rental with my own money, and I felt safe there…as safe as I could with my shadow inciting constant paranoia. Zach hadn't made a peep in over six months. Jax assured me I was safe from him, but he refused to tell me what had become of my brother, and I didn't want to think about it long enough to speculate. A person could go nuts thinking about this shit.

I pulled into the driveway and silenced the engine, wiped my eyes, then pushed the car door open. Placing one boot on the cement, I stepped lightly so I wouldn't slip on ice before taking cautious steps toward the front porch. But when I raised my eyes, the world came to a standstill. Someone had tacked a note to the door. With trembling fingers, I unpinned it and slowly unfolded the piece of paper.

I'm coming for you.

The note fell from my hands, and I stared at the doorknob as if it would jump out and bite me. Those were Rafe's words.

His.

But he wasn't coming back. I hadn't wanted to accept it, but I had, so that only left one other option. Someone else was threatening me. Maybe one of the men from the underground had escaped the police. What if they'd missed the one bad guy who would find me and do the unthinkable?

Or…what if Zach was here to take me again? He could have gone into hiding, watching and waiting until I let down my guard—until there was no one left to stop him, not even our screwed up dad.

But those words...

Someone was playing with my head. Grinding my teeth, I jammed my hand into my purse and pulled out my gun and keys. This was going to end, one way or another. I jerked the key toward the knob but missed. After two more impatient, freaked-out attempts, I inserted the key and turned.

The door was unlocked.

Oh God.

I retreated, and a slow tingle of dread overtook me. Someone was already inside my house. Waiting. Hunting. I swallowed the acidic taste of vomit, gripped the gun handle tighter, and gave myself a mental push forward. I wedged the door open with the toe of my boot, certain I'd locked it, just as I was certain I'd left the light on near the entrance. The shadows of late afternoon screamed at me to run in the opposite direction. I warred with myself, the saner part demanding I get into the car and find a safe place, but I was tired of running.

I'd sooner die.

And then there was the masochist in me. The naive girl who believed Rafe was alive and waiting inside. I shook off that clinging hope and crossed the threshold.

"Show yourself," I demanded, voice nowhere near as steady as the hand I used to grip the gun. *That* I knew how to handle. But as I curled my finger around the trigger of death, I questioned if I could kill another human being. No amount of time spent shooting at the range could prepare me for taking someone's life. "Just leave me alone!"

A tall shadow emerged, and I stiffened, my finger twitching on the trigger.

"Leaving you alone isn't an option, sweetheart."

A noisy gasp escaped my lips, and the gun clattered to the floor, forgotten as the shadow morphed into the form of a figure moving toward me, hands reaching. He pushed me against the door, then his mouth was on mine, his tongue forcing my lips open and dipping inside. Seeking. Conquering.

I kissed him back, lost to delirium, to the blend of our moans as our tongues tangled. My world spun from the familiar scent of him, from the solid feel of his chest underneath my palms. He broke away, but his hungry mouth veered to my cheeks, his tongue darting out to catch my tears.

The reality of his presence bubbled in my throat, and I forced his name out with a sob. "Rafe."

"Fuck, how I've craved your tears."

My whole body shook in his arms. I clawed his skin just to convince myself he was here, but all the grief I'd tried burying crashed through and collided with the euphoria of finding him alive in my house. I screamed at him, pounding my fists on his chest, straddling the line between sane and delirious.

"How could you leave me? I fucking hate you!" As quick as my fury rose, it seeped from my bones, and I slumped against him, burrowing my face in his rough denim jacket as I sobbed.

He hefted me into his arms and strode to the couch. We tumbled onto the cushions, where he crouched over me and entrapped my wrists above my head.

"I didn't want to leave."

"Why did you? *Why?*"

"I wanted you to be safe from…" He let out a sigh, shoulders slumping. "I wanted you to be fucking happy."

"Do I look happy?" I said, glaring at the shadow of his face.

"You look pissed."

"You let me think you were dead! It's been six months. Six months!" If he hadn't pinned me, I would have slugged him. I fisted my hands, aching to slam into his face, to make him feel the slightest bit of pain, even if it would never compare to my own.

He leaned down, his hair brushing my temple. "My head was a mess. I wanted to give you a chance at something normal."

"Normal?" I spat through gritted teeth. "I must have failed your test then, huh? Is that why you're here now? You finally figured out I'm as screwed up as they come."

"No, baby. I failed the test."

"What does that even mean?"

"It means I'm done fighting who I am. You belong to me." He let go of my hands, reached into his pocket, and withdrew something. In the shadows of dusk, I could barely make it out, but once I did, my heart took off in a sprint. He held a syringe identical to the one he'd used the night he kidnapped me. God, how that seemed like a lifetime ago.

"You got your memory back," I said, not expecting an answer because I knew it was true. He was darker, harder, no longer caged by the burden of amnesia.

"I remember everything."

"Then you remember that I was okay with being yours." I eyed the syringe, and a hint of fear busted through my defenses. "Why the drugs?"

"You don't wanna be awake for where I'm taking you." He pulled the cap off and held the needle a couple of inches from my neck. "Does that scare you?"

"No," I said, clenching my jaw. I didn't bother inching away from him, even if my skittering pulse gave away the lie.

"You realize I'm never letting you go, right?"

For a few heavy seconds, I failed to breathe. I'd hate him later, would rail and scream and sob until I had nothing left in me. But in this moment, the absolute ownership in those words cast me under his spell.

"You sure about that?" I tilted my head, giving him easy access to my neck, challenging him to mean his oath. To act on it.

"You can count on it," he said, and then he plunged in the needle.

2. CHAMPION

RAFE

This was the moment I normally lived for. The adrenaline rush of knowing I had him. The smell of sweat and blood in the air. The crowd that chanted Rafe "The Choker" Mason. I moved into a kick-jab combo, but the moves glanced off him like pesky flies.

So maybe I had him.

I always faced the chance of an opponent catching me off-guard, or even worse get one up on me. Tonight, both of those outcomes were real possibilities.

Alex's name ricocheted in my mind, drowning out the crowd. There was nothing left in my head but her. No fight, no chaotic mob of people on the other side of the cage. Just Alex knocked out and tied up on my boat near this damn barn.

Fuck, I didn't want to be here. But in all reality, Alex would be safer if I let off some steam before I woke her because getting lost in the silky texture of her skin while strung this tightly…that could be dangerous.

Jax shouted my name above the din, but the warning came too late. A large fist slammed into my forehead, making my head kick back. My opponent sent another strike to my jaw. The distraction of Alex De Luca was going to cost me this fucking fight.

He came at me again, and I ducked at the last second, forcing my head into the fight. Literally. I slammed into him, grappling his massive frame into a body lock, but fuck, he had some furious strength. He escaped the maneuver, and we sprang apart, bouncing on our feet. The bastard's cocky mug blasted me from a couple of feet away. We'd been circling each other for a while now, sizing the other up as tension thickened the space between us.

I got a right hook in then backed off, sensing his next move by the bunch of his shoulders, the way his hawk-like gaze followed my every step. I anticipated him coming, but I was too close to the fucking cage. His momentum hurled me straight into it. As the metal clanked, time seemed to slow. The overhead lights glinted off his bald head as sweat trickled down the side of his scruffy face.

The cage was cold and familiar at my back. I pushed against it for leverage, bringing an arm up and twisting. With a grunt, I took him to the ground and wrapped an arm around his neck, lips pulled tight over my teeth. Adrenaline careened through me in a sudden burst, and he slumped with each pulsating thump of my heart.

This was it.

The *moment.*

Nothing else mattered except the next few seconds when his lids would droop and shutter the realization that he was losing. The ref shouted at me to stop, but I ignored him and increased the pressure on the guy's throat. As I restricted his oxygen, something inside me buzzed, wept with fucking relief. The ref was crazy if he thought I'd back off. I never stopped, and the crowd knew it. They lived for it. My opponents knew it and hoped it wouldn't happen to them, but it always did because there were few rules in this cage.

The ref finally dragged me off him by force. I jumped to my feet, staggering forward, about to hoist the guy's spent body off the floor and demand more. But the ref blocked me and shoved me back, all the while shouting at me to cool off.

It wasn't enough. This fight, my self-inflicted banishment from Alex...I still couldn't protect her.

From me, the violent maniac inside this cage. I wasn't a champion. I was a disgusting excuse for a human being.

I shook off the self-loathing as Shelton, the guy behind this corrupted operation, strode into the cage with his usual swagger. He flung my arm in the air and announced me as the winner in his deep, booming voice that reverberated through the barn. His woman attached herself to his side. She had no business being in here, but she had a habit of hovering. She licked her lips, her brown eyes roaming my abs as she straightened her spine and pushed out her double D's. I couldn't remember her fucking name, and I didn't care to, even if she was the boss' girl.

Only one girl flooded my mind, rushing blood straight to my cock, and she was stowed away on my boat, fucking *safe* from Zach. He was no doubt making a beeline for Portland right now, but we were miles from there in the middle of nowhere, on the edge of a secluded lake. Not many people frequented this area in the dead of winter, which made it the perfect place to engage in illegal fighting. Turned out it was also the perfect place to go off the grid, which I'd gotten fucking good at since I'd left Perrone's estate in flames.

Jax appeared at my side and shoved clothing and a water bottle into my arms. As he took a long drag on his cigarette, I downed the lukewarm water in a single gulp.

"Alex okay?"

"Still sleeping like a baby," he said, exhaling smoke through his nose.

"Thought you were quitting that shit." I gestured at his cigarette with the empty bottle before dropping it in the duffle he'd set at my feet.

"I did, but then I started again." He shrugged. "Don't worry, I'll quit again tomorrow."

With a shake of my head, I snickered. We'd had this conversation for days. I pulled on a pair of sweatpants over my red trunks and eyed the exit.

"So," he said, drawing on the butt one last time before snuffing the end out between two fingers. "I only caught the last few minutes, but it looked like you were off your game. You still nailed it though. Congrats, man." His words rose above the cacophony of voices, the exchange of money and drugs. This place was a fucking pit, and I hated every second of it.

Except for that moment when I choked the fuck out of the sucker in the cage with me. The release of endorphins made it easier to sleep at night. Sometimes, it even chased away the nightmares.

"Another night, another dime," I said. Big fucking deal. I grabbed a towel from the duffle and wiped the sweat and blood from my face. Sliding my arms through the sleeves of a navy blue hoodie, I pushed my feet into a pair of sneakers. My gaze veered to the exit again.

I had more important shit to worry about than tonight's precarious win. I could see nothing but Alex, think of nothing beyond her body restrained on my bed.

Alone and vulnerable.

Holy fuck, I had to get out of here.

"I'll go collect," Jax said. He knew. One look into my wild, feral face, and he knew that I needed to be with Alex on that damn boat. Of course he did—he'd given me the heads up about Zach's escape. I'd pushed ninety the whole way to Portland, my knuckles white on the steering wheel. When she'd walked through that door...

Fuck, relief didn't even begin to describe it.

Adrenaline still pumped through my blood, stringing me so tight I might snap in two. Six fucking months without her had nearly killed me. Fighting in this damn cage tonight instead of being with her was killing me, but I hadn't been able to back out. Not without pissing off some guys no one dared piss off.

I slung the duffle over my shoulder and elbowed a path around people, ignoring congratulatory high fives and murderous glares. The steady din of voices receded, and that fucking door ballooned in my eyesight.

I wanted through it, now. Wanted across the field to the dock where my boat called to me. Where the sexiest temptress on the planet, in the fucking universe, waited with her wrists and ankles bound by leather, body helpless and begging to be stripped bare.

We both knew our true bindings; the invisible line, born of pain and devastation, which connected our hearts. Nothing on Earth could sever that, not even six months, during which I'd tumbled down the path of no return. Even so, I'd known.

Going back for her wasn't an *if*—it was a *when*. But I never thought Zach would be the reason for going back. If not for his escape, I'd still be battling my inner demons and convincing myself she was better off without me. And maybe she was. I considered the various layers between us—space, doors, even the clothes hiding her body. The horrific things I'd done. That last layer was thick and not as easy to overcome as opening a door or ripping material apart. She was going to hate me, not only for what I'd done—leaving her alone and believing I was dead—but for what I wanted to do, the urges I could no longer contain.

Like squeezing the fucking life out of her brother as soon as I tracked down his ass. I should've killed him six months ago. Then it would be done. Over with. No longer an issue I had to agonize about. And I'd never have to worry about him going after Alex again.

My heart pounded in my ears as the exit drew closer. I was mere feet from it when someone grabbed my shoulder. I whirled with a lethal scowl and found Nate, Shelton's lapdog.

"Boss wants to talk to you," he said, pointing toward the back of the barn. "He's upstairs."

Damn it. Swallowing a frustrated sigh, I gestured at Nate to lead the way, figuring Shelton wanted to needle me about my last minute decision to quit fighting after tonight. I followed Nate through the haze of tobacco toward the back of the barn and climbed the stairs to the loft. Shelton stood ramrod straight, his tatted arms crossed as he watched the mayhem from above everyone else.

We'd known each other back in the day when life was simpler. When I'd had a fucking future. Connecting with him again after all these years had been a fluke, yet it couldn't have happened at a better time. I'd come to the area a broken man, a shell of who I used to be, so I could be near my son. Will's grandparents were raising him now, and though I wasn't about to disrupt his life with my toxic presence, I'd needed to see how he was coping after Nikki's death.

I hadn't planned on sticking around long, but then Shelton drew me into his world of underground fighting, and the allure of stepping back into the cage proved too powerful.

But I had no intention of dragging Alex into this scene. It was time to move on, especially now that Zach was free.

"You wanted to see me?" I asked.

Shelton didn't acknowledge my presence until I was practically breathing down his thick neck. His mouth thinned into a line, and his fetch boy must have taken that as a cue to leave because the little shit was already halfway to the staircase. Shelton's shrewd gaze lingered on the people huddled in drunken groups around the cage.

He scratched his nose for a moment. "Still set on leaving all this?"

"I've got other priorities."

"I'm gonna wager Zachariah De Luca has something to do with these sudden priorities."

"You know something I don't?" I asked, wearing my best neutral expression.

"My guys found him sneaking onto the property during the fight. That's what I know."

It was amazing how a single sentence had the power to ice my blood. I spun on my heel, ready to bolt down the stairs, but Shelton grabbed my shoulder.

I shrugged him off. "Alex is alone—"

"She's fine, right where you left her. My guys made sure of it." He stepped back and let out a breath.

I stared at him, slack-jawed. I didn't want to know how he knew that, but he seemed intent on telling me anyway.

"De Luca junior had some interesting things to say, I'll give him that, but I always check shit out. Got a shock when I searched your boat. What are you doing with that girl?"

"Protecting her from him."

He raised a brow. "Looks like you've got a problem then."

I looked around, feeling as if we were being overheard, but everyone was below, lost to the adrenaline left over from the fight. Not to mention the booze and drugs.

"Where's he at now?" There was no point pussy-footing around this. Too much was on the line, mainly, Alex's life.

He cocked his head. "A place where he can't cause trouble." Shelton paused. "I think we can help each other out."

"How so?" A foreboding disquiet festered in my gut.

He turned his back to the crowd, and we moved further into the shadows. "Abbott and I have history. Let's just say we don't get along. He was a fucking power-hungry shark in the biz." Shelton shook his head. "Shoulda been a goddamn bottom feeder."

I let out an obvious sigh. Everyone knew Shelton liked to string people along with his talk, but I didn't have time for his bullshit.

He planted a hand on my shoulder and leaned in. "We got a good thing going here, but the deep pockets are getting antsy. They want something different, something more exciting than you winning every damn match. Since you're wanting to bow out, I need you to do it with a bang."

"Get to the point, Shelton."

"I'll make sure you get your hands on De Luca junior

before your buddy sends him packing to Mexico again."

Damn Jax. Six months ago, he'd gotten to Zach before I could. Weeks later, when he returned a total mess over not finding any leads on his sister, I hadn't had it in me to give him shit for interfering.

I shook off Shelton's hand. "What the fuck do you want?"

He grinned. "It's not what I want. It's what you want. People talk, Mason. I heard you wanted that sonofabitch dead."

"That's my business."

"As long as you're living on my land, fighting in my cage, what you do is my business." He paused, and the weight of that long beat roiled in my gut. "A match between two longtime rivals," he said, raising a brow, "now that's a fight. Personally, I think it's the least you can do."

I didn't like owing people but owe him, I did. If not for him, I wouldn't have a place to dock my boat, a cage to unleash my rage in, anonymity to hide behind. The network knew who I was—kind of hard to hide while fighting before their eyes. But the world at large thought I was missing, and before tonight, Alex had believed I was dead.

But Shelton was asking too much. The only cage Zach deserved to step into was the kind that locked from the outside. "What if I say no deal?"

He swiveled his head from side to side, making his neck pop. "I know you don't want him getting his hands on your girl because of a little thing like pride. If you back out, he wins by default, and the prize for him is freedom."

I jerked forward, barely keeping myself in check. "Do you have any clue what he's capable of?"

"I know what you're capable of. You want a shot at him, well here's your chance." He lowered his voice. "No ref will stop you this time. Not in this match."

I wasn't a killer by nature. At least, I didn't like to think I was. But I protected what was mine, and Alex was mine. I thought of all the hell we'd been through, all the fighting just to fucking survive, and how it all tied back to Zach. I could start another war, make another enemy, or I could do what Shelton wanted and gain an ally against Zach—do what I should have done six fucking months ago.

Terminate an obsession that would never stop coming.

"He's fucking psychotic. I can't risk him coming after Alex in the meantime."

"I've got the situation contained."

I fisted my hands. "I wanna see him."

"You'll see him in the cage soon enough."

"No," I said, giving an indomitable shake of my head. "Until I see the bastard for myself, we don't have a deal."

He ran both hands through his graying hair. If not for that revealing sign, no one would believe he was a day over thirty-five. "Fine. Swing by here tomorrow around noon. I'll have him here."

I pulled in a deep breath to calm my anger. "I thought you were above this shit. This is blackmail, Shelton."

"This is business. So do we got a deal?"

The type of match he had in mind wouldn't be another watered-down fight in the barn. Maybe, if things went my way for once in my fucking life, I could keep Jax from finding out about our arrangement. Zach couldn't be whisked away to a Mexican prison if I killed him first.

With an impatient sigh, Shelton stuck his hand out. "What do you say?"

"Yeah, we've got a fucking deal." I ignored his offer to shake on it. Nothing was set in stone, especially when it came to Zach fucking De Luca.

Shelton's lips curved upward. Anyone not on hyper-alert wouldn't notice that twitch, but it was there. "Thought you'd see things my way. Until tomorrow then."

I took the stairs two at a time, my fear for Alex's safety heightened. I nearly launched myself through the door, but Jax caught up to me as I pulled it open. A draft of chilly air rushed inside, carrying the scent of the ocean. We were several miles inland, but that distinctive part salt, part fish smell infused the air.

"What'd Shelton want?" Jax asked.

I stepped outside and hastened my stride. He followed on my heels, mere paces behind me. I threw a glance over my shoulder. "Nothing to worry about."

We crossed the field toward the dock, our sneakers sinking into land soggy from the downpour of last week. Fog drifted low on the ground, and the constant mist that was more annoying than rain clung to our clothes. I burrowed into my hoodie as the urgency to get to Alex spurred me on. I nearly broke into a run.

"Hey, slow down, man. Where's the fucking fire?"

We approached the dock, and a small niggle of relief tore through me. The boat appeared untouched. I moved down the wooden planks, my feet skidding over the slick surface, and stepped aboard. Preparing for the sway, I let the craft settle under my sneakers before descending the stairs into the cabin, through the galley, past the living area, straight to the bedroom.

To *her*.

I curled my fingers around the knob and turned, my breath stalling in my lungs. A second passed with an ominous preamble, and a million what-ifs nagged me.

What if she was gone? What if Zach had already gotten to her? What if she'd awakened sooner than anticipated and had somehow broken free of the restraints?

What if she fucking hated me?

26

The door creaked open, and all my fears escaped in an exhale that encapsulated the very meaning of the word relief. Right where I'd left her, indeed. I drank up the sight of her like a man dying of thirst. Quiet footfalls sounded behind me.

"Why are you so jumpy?" Jax asked, his voice low as if he sensed the need to whisper. "There's no way Zach found this place so fast."

But he had. How, I didn't know.

Backing away slowly so I wouldn't wake her, I followed him into the galley and went straight for the beer. Jax was always up for a good brew. Shit, after the day I'd had, maybe I was too. I grabbed two bottles from the fridge and handed him one.

"So what's up with Shelton?" he asked, popping the cap.

I did the same with my beer and took a drink before answering him. "He wants to do something different for the next fight." That much was true. "I don't know all the details yet." Also true...sort of.

If I wasn't going completely fucked-up insane, Shelton was hinting that only one of us would walk out of there alive.

Jax drew on the longneck, eyeing me, assessing how much bullshit I was spewing. I wouldn't fool him for long, but hopefully he'd buy it long enough for me to battle Zach in the last match the piece of shit would ever fight.

3. TATTOO

RAFE

I didn't like lying to Jax, regardless of our rocky history, but I didn't see how I had much choice. We stood firmly planted on opposite sides of the fence when it came to handling Alex's brother. After three beers and more silence than either of us could stand, he left. We weren't comfortable with the elephant between us—the one we never spoke of. Last thing I wanted was to stomp all over his pride, so I tried not to rub Alex's presence in his face.

But he knew I was going to fuck her six ways to Sunday.

And I knew it bothered him, but shit, he was the closest thing I had to a friend. To a family, for that matter. Even after the hell he'd put Alex and me through, I couldn't cast him aside. Our bond ran too deep.

Too bad he wanted it to run deeper.

I double-checked the locks, made my way to the bedroom, and peeked at the gun I'd hidden an arm's length from my pillow. Rounding the bed, I came to a standstill at the end. The longer I stood like a statue, my cock hard as fuck as I feasted on the sight of her, the more I wanted to shake her awake.

As if sensing my presence, she stirred, though she couldn't move with her ankles and wrists secured to the anchors on the wall and floor. Grabbing her today had been a last minute emergency, but I'd been preparing for this day for a while, like a paranoid lunatic building a fallout shelter. Except I hadn't been preparing for another threat against us—I'd simply wanted to be ready when the day came that I wouldn't be able to stay away from her anymore.

Not if…when.

So I'd mounted anchors for restraining her, had tucked away whips, paddles, and other implements in drawers—ready to deliver painful strikes—along with clothing and barely-there lingerie. Assuming I let her wear anything at all.

Her low groan brought me back from the dark pit of fantasies that teased from the edges of my mind. The drugs were wearing off, but not fast enough for my liking. I tugged on the chain to the overhead light. Her lids fluttered, revealing two jade eyes that zeroed in on me.

She blinked several times then parted her lips. "Where are we?"

A simple question, untainted by fear or doubt. That's how much she trusted me. Shit, how I wanted to be worthy of her trust. If anyone was fearful here, it was me because six months apart had taught me only one thing; I needed her with every fiber of my sadistic being.

"You're home." I peeled the hoodie from my torso and tossed it on the floor, then I lifted a knee and slowly climbed onto the bed. Crawling over the mattress like a lethal predator, I settled my knees between her spread thighs.

"Where's home?" she asked, chest rising and falling rapidly. Her dark curls trailed behind her in a riot on the pillow. I fisted my hand in those silky locks, keeping her immobile, and teased her mouth with mine. She darted her tongue out to wet her lips. Fuck, she was already killing me, and I hadn't even kissed her yet.

"Your home is underneath me, sweetheart." I inched back, parted her jacket single-handedly, and took in the cleavage peeking from between the unbuttoned collar of her purple top. I couldn't help but wonder how many assholes had raped that expanse of flesh with their eyes as she went about her day.

She pulled at her bindings, her neck straining as she eyed the cuffs trapping her wrists. "Afraid I'll run?"

"I don't know," I said, quirking a brow in challenge. "Will you?" Grabbing her chin, I ran my tongue along the seam of her mouth, but she twisted her head to the side. "You're mad at me," I said.

She scoffed, refusing to meet my eyes. "Hurt, mad. Take your pick, Rafe."

I winced. Hurt was much worse than mad, and she was both. I unlatched the buckles and gathered her hands above her head, telling her without words that she wasn't to move.

And that was the twisted beauty of us—we understood each other without making a sound. She'd lie there and take it, no matter how fucking angry or hurt she was. Silencing a groan, I gripped the collar of her shirt and ripped it down the middle. In the midst of flying buttons, my gaze traveled over the black satiny cups of her bra before coming to a standstill on the white bandage that covered her belly. Rage ignited, so intense and hot it was nearly uncontrollable. I was ready to blister her fucking ass.

"Rule number one," I bit out between clenched teeth. "The only one allowed to hurt you is me." I wrapped my fingers around her throat. Squeezed. Watched her startled eyes grow huge.

Frightened.

Fuck.

Breathing hard, I loosened my grip. I'd learned a lot

about control during our separation, but I wasn't about to push it—not when it came to her.

"Did you cut yourself again?"

"No," she wheezed. "Look underneath."

Keeping one hand clamped around her throat, I slowly peeled back the bandage. Everything inside me combusted. The sight of my name inscribed on her belly, eradicating Zach's claim on her incinerated me. But it went deeper than the layers of her skin. She'd found a way to brand me on her soul. The delicate letters flourished over her stomach, accompanied by butterflies with perfect wings.

She'd found freedom in that ink. Swallowing hard, I met her gaze and cursed the sharp sting of vulnerability in mine.

"I just got the last touch up today," she whispered. "I couldn't let you go, no matter how hard I tried."

Strength failed me. I collapsed onto her belly, my lips brushing over my name on her pale skin, and squeezed my eyes shut. Somewhere inside me, the beast had clawed its way out and now it was snarling, impatient to claim and own. That's why I'd left the note and drugged her. Never mind her phobia of water—at the base of my being I'd wanted to mess with her head, show her that she belonged to me, even if she was a willing captive.

Especially because she was a willing captive. A headstrong, sexy captive with a self-destructive streak I was determined to break. I intended to be a hard ass, a consistent enforcer. She'd have zero fucking wiggle room with me from here on out.

But fuck, I hadn't expected this.

"Thank you," I said, dotting kisses over her stomach, following the path of my name.

"For what?"

"For being mine."

And she was. Fuck she was, even if I didn't deserve her.

4. FRAGILE

ALEX

Being his was the culmination of my life. Even when I became old and gray, assuming I made it that far, I knew his name would be the last vow on my lips, his face the last image in my mind.

I was born to be his.

Until he threw me away again.

I wanted to believe this time would be different. I had no desire to escape him. My prison was beyond Rafe Mason. The world and independence and freedom held nothing but shackles for me. He made me fly. He made me feel alive. Rafe had the power to quiet the hissing between my ears that begged for pain because I knew he could issue it better than I ever could. But could I trust him not to annihilate my world all over again?

For the first time in my life, I was truly fragile. Zach had hurt me for years, but I'd constructed a wall of numbed acceptance to cope. Lucas and his men had tried to destroy me with the strike of a whip and the threat of Rafe's death, but we'd survived. At least, I thought we had until he'd disappeared.

How ironic that the guy who loved me most ended up being the one to break me to pieces.

The soft, warm brush of his lips over my tattoo was so out of tune with the dark thoughts roaring in my head that I had to give myself a mental shake. I was a boneless puddle underneath him, laid out in pure vulnerability. Shell-shocked.

"How long was I out for?"

He lifted his head. "About five hours." His lips curved downward. "I had something I couldn't get out of tonight. Trust me, I wanted to be here with you instead."

Trust him.

But where the fuck was he six months ago? Jax's words echoed from that morning, as clear as if he'd uttered them now.

He didn't make it.

The branded image of him flashed in my mind. Eyes lowered, and his shoulders slumped as soot and blood bathed his face.

There was a fire...I'm sorry...

I'd sat chained to Rafe's bed in that safe house, my voice refusing to work, so all I'd been able to do was shake my head. Denying. Trying to convince myself Jax was a lying bastard, which technically, he was, but somewhere deep inside, I'd known. Rafe wasn't coming back.

Now here he was months later, asking me to trust him as if nothing fundamental had changed between us, but *everything* had changed the instant he'd decided to bolt.

The urge to smack him was overpowering, but I tamped it down. Instead, I feathered my fingers through his dark hair, brushing away a lock and revealing a red gash above his brow. "What happened?"

"Had a fight tonight."

So the ghost of Rafe Mason fighting underground wasn't a ghost after all. "How bad are you hurt?"

"Not as bad as the other guy. Which reminds me…" He pushed to his hands and knees and scooted down the mattress, then rose to his feet. "I'm a mess." He bent and released my ankles. "I want you naked when I come back from showering."

Tingles shot through me, straight to the core of my being. Fear, desire, even fury, and it all coalesced into a boiling pot of turbulence in my stomach. My body wanted him. God how I wanted him. But my mind and heart overruled, reminding me of the nights I'd sobbed into my pillow with a gun in my hand because I was scared of the shadows in the bedroom.

Because I couldn't fucking breathe without him.

"We need to talk." I glared at him. "I'm—"

"Gonna get *naked*," he finished for me. His eyes undressed me with the heat in them, and his inflexible jaw challenged me to fight him.

I wanted to fight him. I wanted to slug him. I wanted to fuck him. But mostly, I *needed* him to explain. "I'm not on birth control anymore," I said, hoping that would be enough to slow him down.

The left corner of his mouth veered up. "I can use your ass just as well, sweetheart."

"Wh-what?"

"I'll be the first, won't I?"

My jaw gaped open, and I managed a stunned nod. No one had done what he wanted to do, and I didn't know how I felt about that. He'd said something similar on the island before everything had blown up in our faces.

"Good," he said. "I'll be the one and only then." He disappeared through a narrow doorway, leaving me frozen on the bed.

Why his immovable attitude shocked me, I didn't know. Everything about this night shocked me, from the instant I'd seen the note on my door to this moment as he switched on the shower.

Rafe was here, just beyond that wall. Naked.

Alive.

And wanting to fuck me in the ass.

I scooted to the end of the bed and pulled my jacket tight. With each movement, a rocking motion made my stomach drop, and a heavy ball of dread formed. I didn't like this. I didn't like this at all.

I tilted my head and gazed around the room. The space was tiny, bordering on claustrophobic, and a musty scent permeated the air. Up near the ceiling, where it connected with the wall, an odd-shaped window sat above the circular anchors Rafe had used to restrain me.

Directly above my head, another anchor threatened all kinds of interesting uses from the ceiling. It matched the ones on the wall. In fact, it matched the two rings on the floor at the end of the bed. They were small, the type of protruding contraption one would stub a toe on if they forgot they were there. He must have installed them because they were a custom touch, asymmetrical to the lines of the room yet aligned perfectly with the bed.

Where had he taken me? He'd said he was drugging me because I wouldn't want to know, but that was akin to waving a red flag in front of a bull. I tiptoed through the narrow doorway, past the sound of water running behind a closed door, and trailed my palm over the table on my right. On the other side, a built-in seating area sat between two rustic wood panels. Ahead, the kitchen was unusually small, the type I'd expect to find in an RV.

Or on a boat.

Sucking in a noisy breath that fractured the quiet, I clung to the metal poll that spanned vertical from the sloping roof to the thin carpeting under my bare feet. Either I was dizzy from the drugs…or the floor was moving. A staircase called to me, daring me to climb and see what lay beyond, but I couldn't get my hands to let go of the bar. The floor swayed again, and I heard his steps an instant before his fingers curled around my bicep.

"What are you doing out here?" His voice traveled down my spine, and for several moments, silence blared through my ears like a reprimand. My limbs stiffened, muscles tensing to keep from shaking. He pried my fingers from the metal and turned me around to face him. Water dripped from his hair, running down his chest, squiggling down the lines of his tattoos. His green eyes drank me up, and the weight of that stare wrapped around me like a blanket, entrapping me in the cocoon of his ire.

"C'mon," he said, tugging me back into the stifling bedroom.

"Can you stop for a minute?" My heart pounded in my throat as I fought his grip.

"What part of naked did you not understand?" He whirled me around and abruptly let go. I stumbled backward and plopped onto the bed.

"The part where you let me think you were dead!

That's the part I don't understand."

He swung his arms out to the sides. "What do you want from me, Alex?"

"I want to know how you could walk away like that? How you could say you love me one minute then fucking disappear the next!"

With a sigh, he lowered his head. "I can't give you an explanation."

"Can't or won't?"

He peeked up through thick lashes. "Won't. You begged for my fucking darkness, well here it is, sweetheart. You've got it."

I studied him, struggling to catch my breath. He was holding something back, something he didn't want me to know. Because he was scared? I folded my arms, all too aware of the sound my jacket made with the movement, and how he wanted it gone along with the rest of my clothing.

"Whatever you're hiding—"

"Who says I'm hiding anything?"

I held his gaze. "The way you're looking at me is telling me you're hiding something. Please, Rafe. I need you. All of you." Like he'd promised, with no walls standing between us. No secrets.

"Please," I begged again in a whisper. "Why'd you do it?"

He stepped forward though he didn't touch me. Not

yet. Slowly, I lowered my gaze to his erection then met his eyes again, wondering if he'd really force anal. The guy who'd kidnapped me all those months ago, before the memory loss, would've fucked me any way he wanted. I saw that guy in Rafe now.

"I did it because I was a spineless dick." He grabbed my chin. "I don't have that problem anymore, so I'll give you one more chance to get naked."

Hurt flared behind my breastbone. "Or what?"

"Don't test me. I know exactly what buttons to push." He ran his thumb over my lower lip before letting go of my chin. We were engaged in a standoff, one I wouldn't win, but I'd be damned if I didn't put up some sort of fight.

Just to piss him off, I took my time shrugging out of my jacket, took even longer removing my tattered shirt. He retreated, giving me room to stand, and it irked me that he didn't seem the least bit bothered by my slow strip tease. I pushed my jeans and panties down my thighs until they dropped to the floor. Carefully, I stepped out of the puddle of clothing, my gaze never breaking from his, and reached behind me to unclasp my bra. The straps slid down my arms, inch by inch until my breasts tumbled free. He pulled his lip between his teeth.

"Lay down," he said, voice thick and raw. "Spread your legs."

"Rafe, please—"

"Fuck, baby." He hissed in a breath. "Keep begging."

His rugged tone knocked the wind from me. Shit, I was in trouble. Swallowing hard, I reclined on the bed and gave him what he wanted, but without the begging part. A cool draft of air danced across my breasts, and I parted my trembling legs. My nipples puckered from the chill of winter that penetrated the walls. My body did the begging for me. For his touch, for his hot mouth sucking my nipples, one then the other, against his tongue.

Heat throbbed between my thighs at just the thought, and most of my anger vanished. I'd merely existed without him. To have him back was overwhelming, exhilarating, and I was aroused as all hell, ready to fly apart at the slightest touch, despite the confusion of emotions all vying for prominence in my heart.

His attention stalled between my spread thighs. "Wider."

Biting my lip, I did as told, bending my knees to fully expose the most private part of myself. "Wide enough?" The words came out breathless, coy even. But I felt far from coy. My heart was pounding so hard and fast I had trouble catching my breath.

He came toward me, one step at a time. "You're fucking perfect." Dark ink rippled over the muscles in his chest, sending me into a trance-like state, and I wasn't prepared for his fingers curling around my ankles. He yanked me to the end of the bed, pushed my legs even wider apart, and plunged a finger inside me.

"So fucking wet already," he said.

"Rafe!" I bowed above the mattress, my hands fisting the blankets.

"I think we need to set some more ground rules," he said, and through the haze of desire clouding my vision, I saw him lick his lips. "Rule number two...you aren't allowed to leave." He slid another finger in and circled my opening.

"Rafe," I moaned, arching into his touch, panting with trying to hold back. "I've never left you. It's been the other way around." He thumbed my clit, and I couldn't bite back another moan. I rode his hand, my body hungering for release, aching for it.

"I'm not talking about that. You're stuck with me, for better or worse. I'm talking about the fact that we're on a boat." He paused and let those words sink in. I'd already guessed as much. "I don't want you setting foot off this thing without me. If you do, I'll chain you to the fucking floor, got it?"

Nodding, I chewed on my lip. He drove me to madness with his fingers, and I moved with him, pushing upward with each plunder. But I couldn't get there. It was like he knew and was doing it on purpose.

"What's the third rule?" I ground out between clenched teeth. There had to be a third rule. There was always a third rule.

"When it comes to me, the word 'no' isn't part of your vocabulary. So when I tell you to get naked, you're gonna fucking strip." He withdrew his fingers, his thumb. God, my clit throbbed for his thumb.

"You ripped my heart out, Rafe."

"I know I did. And you can yell at me all you want. But you're gonna do it naked because that's how I want you."

"So you say jump, and I ask how high? Is that how this is going to work?"

"Yep."

Cocky sonofa—

He thrust his cock into me, and I gasped. The ability to think or speak evaporated. He shoved deep, his girth stretching me wide, impaling me with nothing but him.

God. Rafe Mason was inside me again. I could hardly grasp it, this moment that was too surreal to be real. I pinched the back of my hand just to make sure this wasn't another dream, that I wouldn't jerk awake to find an empty bed and an even emptier heart.

But this was real.

Real.

Propping on his elbows, he leaned over me and stared into my eyes. Barely breathing. Not speaking. Not moving. Just there inside me, rock hard and pulsating.

Driving me fucking insane.

The need for more tore through my chest, closed my

throat, and burned behind my eyes. I squeezed them shut and fought impending tears. He filled me up so much, too much, until there wasn't any room left for myself.

"Rule number four," he whispered, his lips brushing my cheekbone. "Don't ever hold back your tears."

My lids fluttered open, allowing hot, salty drops to trickle from my eyes…allowing him to lap up my pain with a greedy tongue.

"I was dying without you," I managed to say beyond the ache in my throat and the furious despair that dripped down my cheeks. I'd endured six months of facing the stillness of night in the midst of nightmares. He'd promised me the world, but in the end he'd turned it upside down without a thought.

"Me too, baby." His hoarse voice traveled through my body, leaving gooseflesh in its wake. He thrust inside me with two languid slides of his cock, and that's all he gave me before pulling out. He jerked me up by the arms, spun me around, and bent me over the mattress. I gripped the bedding in both hands, my chest heaving with each inhale and exhale, colliding with the sound of his shallow breaths at my ear.

"Do you trust me?"

I wouldn't have hesitated before he'd left, but now all I offered was a nod. A lie.

I *wanted* to trust him.

"Don't move," he said, his tone commanding

obedience.

"Wh-what are you doing?"

"Need lube for this. I don't wanna hurt you."

"You don't have condoms, but you've got lube?"

He brushed my hair to the side, and his lips trailed down my spine. "Sweetheart, I didn't need condoms because you're it for me. I've had six months of nothing but lube, my fucking hand, and a shitload of vulgar fantasies all starring you." He pushed away from the bed, and his confession of celibacy heated me from the inside out. I was relieved yet terrified because I could already tell how worked up he was.

My ass was on the line. Literally. And he'd already said I wasn't allowed to tell him no.

There was no *no*.

Rafe had finally claimed me. My body, my will, my life.

My everything.

5. ELIXIR

RAFE

I was a man obsessed, a man on the brink, and Alex would suffer for it. Even knowing this, I couldn't go back. I'd finally done what I'd thought about doing since I parted ways with Jax amidst the inferno of our destruction.

Alex and I had come full circle. I remembered every touch, every cry of pain, every thrill that stormed through my blood at knowing she was at my mercy. I wanted her there again, unable to get away or deny me anything. As I squeezed the silky, water-based substance into my hand and palmed my cock, the darkness inside me took hold. Potent and undeniable, I couldn't stop this if I wanted to. The idea of slipping into the one place no one had fucked was too tempting.

She must have sensed the near frantic need consuming me because she clenched her ass cheeks and squirmed. I stilled her with a firm hand on her back, and that's when my demons surfaced. My whole body trembled as I gouged my fingers into her skin. But even as I held her perfect ass in my hands, the ghost of Cleft assaulted me. The rapes in prison were never far, always a part of me, no matter how much I tried to bury the memories.

Shuddering, I closed my eyes for a few seconds and eventually came back to myself. To her. She was trembling as much as I was.

"Are you scared?"

"Y-yes."

"I'll be gentle. Get on the bed and tuck your knees under you. I want your ass in the air."

She climbed with a half sob, half whimper. "I'm not ready for this," she said, her voice full of uncertainty. Yet she raised her butt anyway, displaying how easily she'd give in to me—how she'd *always* give in to me.

Grinding my teeth, I smacked her backside hard. "Higher."

She immediately capitulated. I spread her cheeks, fingers teasing the opening of her tight hole I couldn't wait to penetrate, and settled behind her. I dragged my index finger lower and probed her drenched pussy, then slowly withdrew, making her raise her bottom without realizing it because she was too busy chasing my touch.

"You want me to be your first, don't you?"

As a tremor seized her, she gave a reluctant nod.

"Good girl."

"Why are you being like this?"

"Like what?"

"So…cold."

My spirit took a nosedive toward hell, thrashing and screaming the whole way, begging me to save me from myself. She was right, but why I'd succumbed to treating her less than the treasure she was…that I couldn't explain.

"You signed up for this," I said, attempting to divert her with an ill-conceived cop-out, "the instant you said 'stay' on that island. I sure as fuck remember that night."

"You're scaring me."

"You need to understand who I am." She should be scared. Her pleasure would be fought for and earned through her tears and pleas every fucking time. That's what got me harder than fuck. I leaned over her back and brought my mouth to her ear. "Just submit, baby. Everything you're holding onto…let it go."

"What if I can't?"

"I know you can." I worked a finger into her puckered hole. She clenched her jaw, and I withdrew and dipped in a couple more times. If I weren't such a shameless prick, I'd prepare her with a butt plug first, but I couldn't wait. I needed to take her this way—needed it more than anything. I'd dreamed about it obsessively, jerked off at the fantasy the whole time we'd been apart.

The last thing no one had taken from her...it was *mine.*

I angled her face so I could see her eyes. Shit, there were those tears again. As I positioned the tip of my cock and inched into her, I leaned down and dragged my tongue up her cheek, tasting the addictive flavor of her pain. Giving her time to adjust, I waited several heartbeats, ready to explode, to pound my stress away.

To feel her tight around me.

I pushed in further, and she yelped. A man with a heart would have stopped for a few seconds so she could get used to my body invading hers, but I could barely manage to keep my pace slow and steady. I hungered for it too much. I pushed in another inch, eliciting another cry of pain.

"It hurts!"

Even as her muscles sucked me deeper, driving me to total annihilation, I hated myself for the heaving sobs that broke free of her twisted mouth. Her hands formed two tight fists, and she screwed her eyes shut. I was doing this to her, pushing her, being a complete and utter jackass... making her hate me.

Drawing in a breath, I willed my dick to take a

breather. "Baby, you've gotta relax, or it won't stop hurting."

"I can't!" she shrieked. "You're too big." She tried crawling up the bed, making it a couple of inches before I pulled her ass flush with my groin and plunged into her. The scream that tore from her mouth lanced through me. She attempted to escape me again, but I held her captive in my madness, my hands gripping her perfectly round bottom and keeping her exactly where I wanted her.

"Take deep breaths. Relax those muscles."

"Please, Rafe," she sobbed.

I pulled out slowly, opened the bottle of lubricant, and fisted my cock with a wet hand, then I worked my way back inside her, rubbing her cheeks as I settled into a gentle rhythm. "Your ass is mine, no one else's."

Slowly, her body relaxed, despite her hiccupping mewls that broke me to pieces because they reminded me of that fucking underground tunnel. Reminded me of her on her toes, taking the harsh bite of Brock's whip.

Now *I* was the one hurting her, and I couldn't stop, couldn't even grasp why I needed to push her to the breaking point. Not even hunting Brock down and torturing the fucker to death had eased this *thing* inside me.

But she did. Every salty drop glistening on her cheek, every howl of pain quieted the raging river of lunacy storming through me.

She was my elixir to sanity.

And I was showing her the blackness that tainted my soul. I was giving her what she had begged for in that dark tunnel—the guy my amnesia had nearly killed forever.

I wound an arm around her middle, mindful of her tattoo, and brought her upright until we kneeled together on the bed. I was deep inside her, and falling even deeper as she leaned her head back on my shoulder and stared at me with tear-filled eyes. Fuck, her ass felt good, closing around my cock with unbelievable tightness. My gaze lowered to her throat. That expanse of skin tempted me, and I thought about curling my hand around her neck, but something held me back.

The flashes of blood spurting from Perrone's neck; the euphoria of choking every last breath from him. And more recently, the copious amount of adrenaline that had flushed my veins as I meted out what Brock had coming to him. He'd been the only one to escape the police, but he hadn't eluded me.

I couldn't risk losing control with Alex—she meant the fucking world to me, and I wasn't about to endanger her. Not yet.

Maybe not ever.

"I love you," I whispered, my lips nearing hers, my cock nestling a little deeper, making her wince. I searched the green sea of her eyes, hoping I'd find forgiveness for taking her like the monster I was.

But I only saw pain.

I reached for her clit and flicked lightly. Her mouth opened, forming a delicate O. I was about to come, was too fucking close, so I tempered myself and gave her the time she needed to catch up. Her body flushed with impending orgasm as I worked my fingers in and out of her cunt. Even in the dim room, overwhelmed by winter and the shadows of night, the sheen of her pink-tinged skin was unmistakable.

"Crash with me," I said before claiming her mouth, adding pressure to her clit, smothering her throaty cries that didn't speak the language of pain, loathing, or even anger. Those muffled howls were an oath of uninhibited surrender. They were pure fucking ecstasy.

6. WHORE

ALEX

"No!" Rafe thrashed beside me in bed, pulling me from sleep. "Get off of me," he said with an agonized groan. Undeniable pain laced his voice, and his helplessness suspended me in a state of horror.

"Rafe," I said in an urgent whisper. "Wake up." I settled my hand on his shoulder, but he screeched a louder cry. Bolting upright, he lunged for me. His sweaty hands clamped around my neck, unrelenting in their intent. I wheezed a plea and squinted at the doppelganger strangling me. Rafe wasn't unleashing an act of sexual perversion—he was a madman lost to the terror of a nightmare.

"Rafe!" I fought for air, but his hands emanated rage.

Cleft's name bled from his lips with a sob.

"It's me..." I said, barely getting the words out. Entrapped in full panic mode now, I dug my nails into the backs of his immovable hands.

He's going to kill me.

The shadow of his massive form grew smaller, darker. My heartbeat throbbed in my ears, like a slow and steady bass drum counting down the last seconds of my life. I yanked his hair, scratched his scruffy face...

Blackness.

A loud gasp tore from my lips, and I sucked oxygen into my lungs as if I'd never breathe again. Clutching my throat, I coughed as Rafe's hunched form at the edge of the bed crystalized. Through my tears, I watched his expression crumble. Tugging the sweat-drenched strands on his head, he shuttered his gaze.

"I-I'm sorry," he said, huffing rapid breaths.

"What"—I coughed again—"happened?"

He ran a trembling hand down his face then stared at me with tortured green eyes. "I was dreaming..." He exhaled in a rush. "I could've fucking killed you."

I swallowed hard, one hand still massaging my throat, and scooted into a semi-reclined position. Somewhere between passing out and coming to, he'd switched on the light.

"What were you dreaming about?"

That's when he shut down. We could have been

sitting in pitch black, and I still would have sensed him withdrawing.

"Doesn't matter," he said, looking somewhere over my shoulder.

"You mentioned Cleft."

"I don't remember." He reached overhead and tugged on the chain to the light, sending the room into darkness again. The mattress shifted under his weight, and his trembling arms enclosed me, urging me to lie back on the bed. Burying his nose in my hair, he settled his body over mine. "I didn't mean to hurt you."

"But you did." I wasn't talking about the choking or even the anal sex. By the heavy moment of silence that fell upon us, I figured he knew that.

"I don't deserve you, Alex. I should let you go, but I can't."

"I'm not asking you to let me go. I'm just asking you to be honest with me."

"I'll end up destroying you."

My heart nearly stopped. That statement was too close to what he'd said in my nightmare while we were trapped in that tunnel. Part of me was scared he was right. The way he'd taken me tonight, forcing his cock in my ass...the residual pain of that pinged through my chest. Then to wake up to him choking me, *really* choking me as if he meant it and wouldn't stop. As if he couldn't stop. He'd spit out Cleft's name while in the throes of his nightmare, all the while squeezing the life out of me. Those were the actions of a tortured man.

"After you left," I began, hesitant because I wasn't sure how receptive he would be to what I was about to say, "I started seeing a therapist. Maybe talking about what Cleft did will—"

"We're not talking about the past. We're moving forward."

"This isn't moving forward."

"Leave it alone," he warned, maneuvering until we were on our sides. He spooned me and grabbed my breast with one hand while the other wedged between my thighs.

"No," I said, a challenge in my tone. "I won't leave it alone. You can't shove everything under the rug and pretend it didn't happen."

"You just broke the third rule, sweetheart." He slid a leg between mine, opening me for his plundering touch. "If you break the rules, you get punished."

Like the whore I was, I spread for him, despising myself for wishing he'd push that finger deeper. "This is your idea of punishment?"

"Yep," he whispered, touching me more fully, his breath heating my ear. He forced his free hand between my lips and depressed my tongue until I gagged. "Fuck, you turn me on so much," he said, thrusting devious fingers in and out of my pussy. "So fucking wet." He pushed against my backside with a grunt.

I bucked into his hand, moaning my pleasure around the fingers that gagged me, drenching the fingers that fucked me. Shameless, I pleaded for him to let me come in muffled whines, inaudible whines, yet he somehow understood them.

Understood them enough to yank his touch from the wet, throbbing place that ached for release.

His fingers slipped from my mouth, and our torturous desire for each other blasted the room in shallow breaths. Tears wandered down my cheeks. Frustrated, angry tears. He wasn't being fair. I moved against his thigh, sliding in my wet need, but he removed his leg. Gathering my wrists in one hand, he held them in front of me, far away from my throbbing pussy.

"Are you gonna tell me no again?"

I almost shook my head until I realized it was a trick question. Instead, I pressed my legs together, willing the space between to simmer down. As if my stillness taunted him, he jammed a finger between my thighs and teased my slit. I arched into his erection, unable to stop myself, and rubbed my ass against his length. Just baiting him, probably playing with fire. He dipped a thumb inside me before wedging it between my lips.

The way Zach used to, except my reaction was vastly different. I sucked my arousal off, quieting a frustrated groan. Rafe would keep me strung all night. I dreaded it, but I also lived for it, knowing how his mind games heightened the thrill. The thought of being trapped by orgasm denial made me squirm. God, I was on the cusp of splintering.

"Do you want my cock in your ass again?" To emphasize the threat, he inched his tip into my tender hole.

I nearly shook my head, almost told him no.

Another trick question.

Going completely still, I counted, drawing in even breaths through my nose. He brushed his fingers over my nipple, and I bit my lip hard to keep from moaning out loud.

"Good girl."

He shifted until the tip of his cock nudged my pussy, and I thought I'd die. How could he hold back so well? Especially since he was as worked up as I was. His chest pressed against my back in a furious tide, and I imagined his mouth stretched tight to withhold a curse. He couldn't hide what his body wanted. His heavy breathing and hard cock gave him away.

He nipped my ear, and his lazy caress on my nipple turned to a hard pinch. "You're so intuitive, knowing when to submit without a single word. So fucking perfect." He tongued the rim of my ear, and I broke out in shivers.

"No more questions. Are we clear?"

No. We weren't clear at all. Somehow, I'd find out why he'd left the way he had. I wouldn't stop until I got him to talk to me. Otherwise, this would never work if we kept secrets from each other—if we couldn't compromise. If we lied to each other.

But he'd left me no other choice. The word no wasn't allowed in my vocabulary, so with my body on fire, held captive by my unwavering need for him, I told him what he wanted to hear.

"We're clear."

7. FAVOR

RAFE

I'd been holding her for hours, comforted by the steady sound of her breathing. Maybe insomnia was a blessing, considering what I'd nearly done to her. If I hadn't woken up when I had...a shudder tore through me, and I held on a little tighter.

My sleep-choking tendencies posed a problem, and one I couldn't ignore. How the fuck was I supposed to fall asleep next to her every night if it meant risking her life?

Mid-morning rays trailed through the tiny window above us. Fuck, I didn't want to leave this bed. Her curls were everywhere; in my eyes, teasing my lips, tickling my face. My fingers were everywhere; snuggled in the folds of her beautiful cunt, brushing a nipple. I spooned her from behind, trying hard not to stroke her awake. If that happened, I'd end up fucking her, and I couldn't do that until I made damn sure she was taken care of. I would not put her in the position of needing an abortion like Zach had. I might not be able to control what I did in my sleep, but preventing an unplanned pregnancy was in my control.

Being careful not to wake her, I slid my fingers from her wet pussy. She sighed, stretched, then settled back into sleep. Something inside me filled to the brimming point. I never imagined I could love someone so much, or so fucking possessively. The urge to pull out the cuffs made my hands twitch.

I liked her helpless.

I liked her *mine*.

Biting back a groan, I eased from the bed. She was mine—that wouldn't change—but things were never that simple. I was still keeping so much from her, stuff she sensed, if her stubborn questions from last night were any indication. I'd killed. I'd lost myself to mental obliteration. I'd erected a wall I wasn't sure even she could hurdle.

The boat swayed, and I held my breath, worried the motion would draw her from sleep. But she didn't rouse. I pulled on my sweats and recalled how I'd kept her in sweet agony for most of the night. It had been a fitting punishment—one that distracted her from giving me the third degree. Truth was, I didn't know if I'd ever be able to talk to her about my time in prison. Even before I'd lost my memory, I'd buried that part of my past under the single-minded focus on getting my hands on her.

I tiptoed from the bedroom, leaving the door cracked open so I'd hear when she awoke though I didn't expect her to rise for a while. After last night, she was going to need her sleep. And I needed something else so I could be with her the way I needed to be with her. As I turned on the coffee pot, I dialed Jax. Wedging the phone between my shoulder and ear, I tapped my fingers on the counter as the call rang through.

He croaked something incomprehensible after the fifth ring, then he coughed and cleared his throat. "What?"

"Good morning to you too," I said, clenching and unclenching my fists three times to release tension.

"Sorry," he mumbled. "Didn't sleep well."

He was preaching to the fucking choir.

"So what's up?" he asked.

"I was wondering if you could do something for me."

"Depends."

"Any chance you can you get your hands on some birth control?"

A lengthy pause ticked by. "I think I can manage that."

"Thanks," I said, watching as coffee began dripping into the carafe.

More silence. "So," he finally said, "guess what Nate told me last night after I left your boat?"

My eye twitched, but I kept my tone neutral. "What'd he say?"

"He said you and Shelton are getting into something lucrative."

Fuck. People and their big mouths.

I must have muttered the obscenity out loud. His dry laughter filtered through the phone. "Funny how I had to hear it from a fucking stranger."

"What else did he tell ya?"

"I know Zach's involved. Is that what you're worried about?"

Basically, yeah.

"You need to put a stop to this," he said. "You're gonna get yourself thrown back in jail, or worse."

"What do you expect me to do? Zach wouldn't be a problem if you hadn't carted him off to Mexico."

"You want to kill him? *Fine*. I won't stop you this time. But shit, man, don't be stupid about it. Don't do it in front of a bunch of witnesses."

"Shelton's already got him. I'm supposed to see for myself at noon. I was hoping you'd keep an eye on Alex while I'm gone."

"This is fucked up," Jax said. "Do you really trust

Shelton?"

"I don't have much choice. He's playing hardball."

He cursed under his breath. "If you go through with this fight…how do you expect to come back from that? This is Zach we're talking about. Not Brock, not even my old man. He's Alex's fucking brother, for chrissakes."

"You came back from what went down in that tunnel just fine." I pointed out as I set a mug next to the coffee pot. "You killed your own blood, so who the fuck are you to lecture me?"

"We're not the same. I did what I needed to. I was born from a slave and raised in that ditch. But you…" He let out a sigh.

"Say what's on your mind, Jax. Wouldn't want to stop you now."

"You've got a fucking huge ass conscience, whether you want it or not."

I bit down on my lip hard. Part of me agreed with him, and it wasn't because I cared what happened to Zach; I cared about what Alex would think of me.

"You're right," I said. "It's complicated." She might be able to look past me choking Jax's uncle in prison, could maybe even forgive that moment in Perrone's estate when I'd snapped. And Brock…well shit, Perrone's most brutal thug had tortured her, only she didn't have an emotional attachment to him like she did Zach and me.

But with Zach…there was only one way to make sure

he never came for her again, and I was positive she would hate me for it. Jax sure as fuck didn't approve. He believed killing Zach would tip me over the edge, that I'd lose the last bit of humanity I still possessed if I killed someone I'd once considered my best friend.

"Complicated doesn't even touch it," Jax said as if he'd heard the internal battle firing in my synapses. "You and Zach have history."

"Zach's not the one I'm worried about. Something kept her quiet all those years. I'm not convinced she was only thinking of me. She even admitted to getting off on it."

"He's her brother, not the love of her life. You know as well as I do that you've got her whipped."

My mouth thinned into a line. "I don't know, Jax. There's a fine line between love and hate. She threw me in that place for eight years because he told her to. That's power."

"And I thought I carried baggage," he grumbled. "You've spent too much time alone in your fucked up head."

"Probably," I said.

"No probably about it. You've been a fucking robot these past six months. You need her. She needs you. I get that. But if you need to take care of Zach, then don't be a dumbass about it. "

Jax always gave it to me straight. Maybe the real

problem was I wanted her to want him dead—it would make this much easier. But my gut told me she'd want to spare his life because she wasn't a fucked up killer like me.

Doesn't matter what she wants.

I was in control now, and no one was going to stop me this time, not even Jax. I refused to make the same mistake of leaving Zach alive—it was the only way Alex would be rid of him for good.

8. TEASE

ALEX

Rafe's quiet voice interrupted the blissful, orgasmic dream I was having. I whimpered, wishing I could stay in the dream where his magic hands explored every inch of my body. I forced my eyes open and blinked several times, despite the scratchiness of my lids. Ugh. He'd kept me in a state of near euphoria for most of the night, my wrists clamped in one hand while he fondled my breasts with the other. I couldn't remember the exact moment I'd relaxed enough to sleep, but once I fell into the dark pit of slumber, I'd managed to find oblivion.

Until now.

I sat up, my elbows depressing the mattress, and blinked again. Words spoken in low tones filtered in from beyond the ajar door. Soundlessly, I slid from the mattress until my feet touched the floor. I was naked, my body on full display from the beautiful tattoo that covered my belly to the ugly battle scars of my life, forever etched into my arms. I crossed them and tried to ward off the chill. My body missed his already, especially his warmth because it was freezing in here. I crept across the room, my teeth chattering, and stood like a statue behind the door, my heartbeat accelerating in my ears as Rafe's words knocked the breath from me.

"Something kept her quiet all those years," he said. "I'm not convinced she was only thinking of me. She even admitted to getting off on it."

A few beats of silence passed before he spoke again. "I don't know, Jax. There's a fine line between love and hate. She threw me in that place for eight years because he told her to. That's power."

He was talking about Zach. I covered my mouth, the full context of his words sinking in. He was talking about Zach *and* me. Obviously, Rafe still blamed me for the hell I'd put him through. I thought he'd forgiven me, but maybe some things couldn't be forgiven. I trailed my fingers over my throat, remembering the unrelenting grip of his fingers. His nightmares were my fault, would *always* be my fault. I pulled the door open and winced at the creak that sounded.

Rafe set his cell on the counter. "Morning," he said,

pouring what looked like strong coffee into a mug. His gaze lingered on me as he took a sip.

Parting my lips, I tried to say something.

What are you not telling me? Why were you talking about my brother?

Even a simple good morning would do, but my vocal cords locked up. My attention narrowed to the dreary light filtering through the small windows, and the fact that we were on a boat grabbed hold of my phobia. Unable to catch my breath, I stumbled into the table. All I could think about was the water surrounding us from outside these walls. Just mere slabs of wood separating us from the suffocating threat of drowning, of darkness and nothingness.

Rafe plopped his mug onto the counter and a bit of liquid splashed over the rim. His footsteps rumbled toward me.

"You're safe," he said, grabbing my biceps with two strong hands. "There's no need to panic. Just breathe." He pushed me with surprising gentleness onto the bench seat.

I sucked air into my lungs, but I couldn't quite reach that spot deep within that burned for a full breath. "I-I can't."

He leaned over me, planted one hand on the table, and lifted my chin with the other. "Babe, I'd never let anything happen to you." His eyes searched mine, though what he was looking for, I couldn't say. Evidence that I wasn't on the verge of freaking out? Trust? "I'm gonna kiss you, and you're not gonna think about anything but me, okay?"

I managed a slight nod before his mouth slanted over mine. His tongue plundered, seeking my surrender, further stealing my breath. He made me forget that I *needed* to breathe.

The water didn't matter. Nothing mattered except him kissing me.

"Better?" he asked, his voice rough and laden with want.

"I don't need to breathe when you're kissing me like that."

"Good," he said, taking my mouth again and running a hand through my tangled hair. His kiss, his touch, the way his voice washed over me—everything about him induced a sense of calm, and I almost forgot about the upsetting phone call I'd overheard. Almost.

I inched back and met his eyes. "I overheard you on the phone. What's going on with my brother?"

His brows curved downward with displeasure. "Nothing you need to worry about." He slid into the seat across from me and averted his gaze. I despised this unbearable weight of tension. Things were different now, only I didn't understand why. We'd survived so much together, had sacrificed so much for each other, yet he wouldn't let me in.

"Why are you shutting me out?" I asked, my palm gliding across the cold surface toward his. The quaking winter chill had subsided, thanks to the space heater I spied emitting a flow of warmth from the galley. But I needed his touch—needed a different kind of heat deep in my belly from being wanted, loved…trusted.

"You know what you need to know. Has nothing to do with shutting you out." He folded his fingers around mine, his green eyes simmering as he lifted my hand and sucked a finger into his mouth.

"Rafe," I whispered, squeezing my thighs together.

"Is that sweet pussy still wet?" Licking his lips, he released my hand. Damn. I fell into submission with a delicious shiver that had nothing to do with the cold. That tingle traveled from the follicles on my scalp to the soles of my feet. How did he do this to me? Every. Fucking. Time.

"You're not gonna tell me what's going on, are you?" I hated the way my voice came out weak and pathetic. Breathless. He had me. He knew it. I knew it.

"Stand up," he said.

"Rafe?"

"I said stand up." He raised a brow in challenge.

Rising on shaky legs, I crossed my arms. "Happy?"

One corner of his mouth lifted. "Not yet." He patted the tabletop. "Get your sexy ass up here. Let's do something about that ache you're trying to hide."

Holy shit. My ability to articulate an intelligent sentence vanished. I slid onto the table, and he pushed me into a reclining position then urged my legs around his shoulders. I braced my palms on the back of the bench where I'd sat, my head hanging over the edge of the table, and tried not to dwell on how he was using sex as a diversion.

He slid his hands up my inner thighs, and I was lost as his fingers parted my folds.

"You want me to taste you?"

I squirmed under his hands, under the hot flush of his breath on my pussy. "Yes…please."

"I'd do anything for you. You know that, right?"

I did know that. He'd risked his life for me, but would he share what made him vulnerable? Would he unburden his fears and let me help carry the weight? I longed for his trust as much as I longed to feel his cock inside me.

"Why did you leave? Help me understand." For the first time in my life, I felt like I was the strong one.

He reached for something behind him. "Take this," he said, rolling an apple over the ink of his name, between my heaving breasts. I caught it before it fell to the floor, one hand bearing my weight for a few precarious moments.

"Why?" I eyed the red apple.

"Bite into it, and keep your hands on that seat. If you

drop the apple, I'll stop licking your cunt."

I chomped into the peel and gagged myself with the fruit as his tongue darted over my clit. Holding onto the back of the seat for dear life, I moaned and moaned and moaned some fucking more, and my teeth sank a little deeper into the apple. He teased my pulsating bud of nerves until I thought I couldn't handle another round, yet I chanted *please don't ever stop* in my head.

Rafe's tongue was my downfall.

If I had an apple wedged between my lips, then I couldn't ask questions. If he drove me out of my mind with his hot, wet mouth on my pussy, then I wouldn't care that he refused to answer. No one could bend me so well, could take more than I wanted to give and make it seem like it had all been my idea to begin with.

His tongue burrowed deep then surfaced to flick and tease. He alternated between making me want less... making me want more. I arched my back, stranded between sweet agony and just plain agony. What a contradiction. He pushed a finger into my center, and I bucked off the table with a cry. I almost lost the apple.

"Easy, sweetheart." His warning vibrated on my throbbing clit. Using my feet, I pushed against the seat cushions behind him and braced my arms for more traction, trying to ride his face. He withdrew, and I screeched my outrage around the apple dripping from my lips. Sweat broke out on my naked body, bowed over the table, legs spread wide in unabashed glory.

He'd reduced me to a shameless hussy, and I was ready to break in two if he didn't stop torturing me.

The boat swayed, shifted, and heavy footsteps announced someone's arrival. "I see I'm interrupting breakfast."

Jax. Shit. I tightened my stomach muscles, bringing myself upright, but Rafe placed a firm hand on my belly that kept me sprawled.

"Don't move. He's seen it all before."

Embarrassment made my skin feverish, and I despised how my chest heaved from my arousal, how my nipples were achingly erect. One look between my legs would be evidence enough; I was Rafe's whore, the one he had no qualms leaving in a state of heightened near-orgasmic state for his buddy to gawk at.

Rafe lifted my leg, scooted over so he could stand, then set my foot on the seat back again. Jax stared at me from the narrow path between the table and couch area, his eyes alight with amusement.

"An apple...that's creative, man."

Creative and messy. Juice trailed down my face toward my ears, and there was nothing I could do about it unless I wanted to risk disobeying Rafe.

Which I didn't.

Rafe leaned against the edge of the table and faced Jax. He wore dark gray sweats that hung low on his hips, and that soft material did little to hide his cock. His erection tented his pants though he didn't seem to care. I couldn't stop staring. I'd give anything to pull the waistband down and take him in my mouth, tease him to death the way he was teasing me.

"You're early," he told Jax.

"You've been too busy eating pussy to pay attention to the time. It's almost noon."

"Fuck." Rafe pulled the apple from between my teeth, then he reached around Jax and grabbed a sweatshirt from the sofa. "I better get a move on." He pushed his arms through the sleeves and pulled it over his head, leaving his dark hair a sexy mess.

Jax's brown gaze swerved between Rafe and me. "Dude, get some clothes on her. I'm not standing watch while she's like that." His harsh tone suggested he was unhappy about more than just my state of undress.

"Go get cleaned up." Rafe helped me to my feet before twirling me in the direction of the bedroom, but I didn't budge. He smacked my ass, and I glared at him over my shoulder.

"You're really gonna leave it like this?" I lowered my gaze to his erection to make my point. I didn't want him to leave. Clearly, Jax wasn't happy about it either. Whatever was going on…it left a bad taste in my mouth.

"I can wait," Rafe said. "The question is, can you?"

He was having too much fun taunting me. "Is this a

game to you?"

"I can make it a game, but you won't win." He gestured toward the bedroom. "There's clothes in the second drawer."

"Where are you going?" Panic laced my voice. I couldn't hide it any more than I could vanquish the dread in my gut.

Please take me with you. Let me in. Don't leave me in the dark.

"I've got something to take care of." He gave Jax a significant look rife with a secret I wasn't privy to.

"If anyone gives you trouble," he told Jax, "you know where my gun is."

9. RUN

ALEX

"You won't tell me what's going on either, will you?" I asked Jax after Rafe had disappeared up the stairs, and the boat stopped moving from his exit. Raising a brow, I crossed my arms over my breasts to hide them. I pressed my thighs together, realizing that standing buck-naked in front of a man other than Rafe was ludicrous.

"Not my place, sorry." Jax slid into the seat Rafe had vacated. Just thinking of Rafe's mouth between my thighs flushed me, and I felt my face go hot.

Jax cocked his head with a smirk, and I swore he knew what I was thinking. "Go put on some fucking clothes, okay?"

He wasn't going to tell me shit. I'd figured as much,

but I'd had to give it a shot. I backed toward the bedroom though I had no intention of doing what I was told—not so long as Rafe insisted on shutting me the fuck out. After everything we'd been through together, I deserved more than that. I let that sink in for a moment. Possibly, for the first time in my life, I not only thought I was worth something, but I believed it.

I enclosed myself in the room. Glancing at the knob, I gritted my teeth and silently cursed. No lock. The weight of time drove me, and I raided the drawers, my heart galloping behind my ribcage as I pulled out a pair of jeans. I couldn't find any panties—not even the black satin underwear I'd removed myself the night before. In fact, all of my clothes were gone, and I had no clue what he'd done with them.

The door whispered a taunt as I jammed my legs into soft denim. Forgoing a bra, I shrugged into a long-sleeved shirt, wedged my sockless feet into a pair of sneakers, and almost expected Jax to bust into the room.

Just breathe.

Five in, hold, five out. Repeat.

The door remained shut. I listened for what seemed like forever, but I couldn't hear anything beyond the erratic pulse thrumming in my ears. I continued my search, sliding drawer after drawer open, sifting through Rafe's socks and underwear, pants, sweatshirts, and gym clothes—even silky, lacy lingerie in dark and sexy colors.

That drawer could be fun. I pulled open the one I had yet to snoop through and my breath stalled.

Rafe had plans for me, all right.

A treasure trove of whips and paddles, dildos, clothespins, and other items I couldn't even name lived in that drawer. He even had a standard set of handcuffs in there. I grasped the cool metal, digging beneath other perverted paraphernalia, and that's when I discovered my purse buried at the bottom. I freed it along with the cuffs amongst a ton of clatter, and my feet carried me across the tiny space with quiet, swift steps. I dropped the stuff on the mattress and dug through my purse, hoping I'd find my gun until I remembered that I'd dropped it in my foyer after finding Rafe in my house.

But he had a gun. I knew he did. He'd even mentioned it to Jax. Considering Rafe would want quick access in the event of an emergency, I figured he kept it close by when he was most vulnerable—while he was sleeping. I rifled through the built-in nightstand next to the bed, but unless I wanted to beat someone to death with a sci-fi novel, I was out of luck.

Shit. I slammed the drawer shut in frustration then went still, on hyper-alert for the thump of footsteps coming my way. Surely Jax heard this racket? Each second I stood in this room, essentially trapped, seemed to take a minute off my life.

The open space beneath the drawer in the nightstand

drew my attention. Acting on a hunch, I ran my hand underneath, palm side up, and my fingers smoothed over the cool handle of a pistol.

Jackpot.

I grabbed my purse and the cuffs, tiptoed toward the door and turned the knob, then stepped in full view of Jax. He looked up, halting mid-bite into a sandwich, and arched a brow at the gun I pointed at him. The sandwich flopped onto his plate.

"If I'd known you were gonna hold me at gunpoint, I wouldn't have made you lunch," he said, gesturing toward the untouched plate sitting across from him.

Food was the last thing on my mind. "You're gonna tell me where he went." I raised the gun a little higher.

He blinked, and his face relaxed into his normal, non-worried expression. But he should be worried. I might not shoot him in the head, but I was at the end of my rope. Jax was going to give me answers, or he might need a sling for his arm in the near future.

"Start talking."

He let out a sigh that ruffled his shaggy hair. "You're not gonna shoot me."

"You sure about that? Maybe I've snapped." I cocked the gun. "Maybe I'm done being a fucking doormat, Jax. A victim. Now tell me where he went!"

"He went to the barn," he said, running his hands through his hair. "Nothing for you to worry about."

I scoffed. "Funny, that's what he said."

He rose from the bench slowly, keeping his eyes on the gun the whole time. "Hand it over. You're being irrational."

Oh hell no. If there was one thing a man needed to learn, it was that he *never* accuse a woman of being irrational. I stuck the barrel to my head and finally got the reaction I was hoping for.

Jax lurched forward with genuine fear in his eyes. "Alex—"

"How's this for irrational?"

"You've gotta be fucking kidding me. I didn't sign up for this shit." He gestured toward the weapon. "Put the damn gun down."

"I'm going after him, whether you like it or not."

"Why the fuck are you doing this?" he shouted.

"He's not acting like himself!" This version of Rafe was more unstable than usual because he was bottling up his demons, and I was terrified of what he'd do when he finally exploded. I tossed the metal handcuffs I'd taken from Rafe's kink drawer onto the table. "Cuff yourself to that pole," I said, indicating the metal rod that separated the sitting area from the galley.

He picked up the cuffs and dangled them by a finger. "C'mon. Be reasonable. You and I both know you aren't going to fire that gun."

"Do you really wanna find out?"

He let out a few colorful words before grudgingly complying. After he'd trapped the pole between his arms with his hands shackled on the other side, I edged past him and ignored the icy glare he sent my way.

"You have no fucking idea what you're doing. Rafe is gonna make you pay for this, and when he does, I'll be there watching."

Stowing the gun in my purse, I took off toward the stairs and grabbed an oversized hoodie I assumed belonged to Rafe on the way, pushing my arms through the sleeves as I climbed the steps. Reality hit me with paralyzing force the instant the wind hit my face, putrid with the scent of fish and fresh saltwater.

Months had passed since I'd tested my ability to overcome my phobia. It wasn't like riding a bike or catching up with an old friend—things a person could pick up months or even years later as if no time had passed. The longer I spent away from facing my worst fear, the harder it was to overcome when the need arose.

And I needed not to freeze now. Sickness boiled in my stomach, and I wanted to slap Rafe silly for taking off, for doing God knows what without telling me what the hell was going on. I earned each step toward the side of the boat through deep breaths, plenty of chanting, and even a few blind stumbles as I squeezed my eyes shut. I didn't remember alighting from the boat, but the trek down the dock brought on a panic attack. I sank to the damp wooden planks, my palms sliding in the moisture from the drizzle of Pacific Northwest rain, and willed myself into a state of tunnel vision. Nothing else existed except that field, just mere feet away.

Jumping to my feet, I sprinted across the slick surface and skidded into the muddy grass. Shit, I didn't have time for this. Rafe had at least twenty minutes on me. Probably longer. Pushing to my feet again, I searched the area, eyes scanning the field for the barn. Through the fog, I made out a brown structure that rose higher than most outbuildings, so I assumed I'd find him there. Doing what, I didn't know.

Those cuffs should hold Jax for a while, but it didn't matter. I still had the gun tucked away in my purse, and I'd threaten to shoot anyone that tried stopping me. My tiny frame swam in the hoodie, but the larger size only aided in hiding my face. A lazy gust of wind teased the hood, and I tugged it low over my forehead. Picking up my pace, I headed toward the barn, and the building grew bigger as I approached.

A door in the front stood ajar. I tiptoed toward it, my back stiffening as male voices filled the air. I recognized Rafe's instantly, but a second voice, tone deep and even, wasn't familiar at all. Then I heard my brother speak, and a chill rivaling the temperature crawled down my spine.

"I don't have a problem with these terms at all."

A scuffle sounded, and when I risked peeking

through the crack in the door, I saw two men holding Rafe back from Zach. He swung his fists anyway and missed Zach by a few inches. My brother stood between two additional men, but his hands were cuffed behind him so he couldn't defend himself.

"Of course you don't have a problem with it," Rafe said, one lip curving upward in a sneer. "You sick piece of shit. You fucking wrecked her." He spit on Zach's sneakers. "I'll die before I let you get your hands on her again."

"Hmm," Zach said, tilting his head, appearing unfazed by the spittle on his shoes. "Yeah, I don't have a problem with that either."

"Enough." A man cut the air with a firm hand, and the way everyone grew silent, I figured he was the guy in charge. "How about we calm down and have a civilized conversation?" He swung his gaze between Rafe and Zach. "I get it. The two of you got issues. But that's what the cage is for. Work it out there."

Rafe glowered at him. "I don't care who the fuck you are, Shelton. You're not involving Alex in this."

"That ain't for you to decide. We're playing on my turf, so we're playing by my rules. You and De Luca junior here will each have a fair shot in the cage. Winner walks away with a hundred grand and the girl, and that's my final word on this."

"Like I said," Zach said, tilting his chin up. "I don't

have a problem with this plan. Better than rotting in that Mexican prison." He glared at Rafe. "Thanks for that, by the way."

"I'll pass on your regards to Jax. If I had my way, you'd be a fucking corpse. You might rethink your decision to escape after I'm done."

"C'mon now." Shaking his head, Shelton stepped between Rafe and Zach. "Let's just call this a settled matter and get on with it, hmm?" He gestured to his men, and they let Rafe go.

Rafe stepped back, cracking the tension from his neck. He was the picture of cooperation, but I knew him too well. He could strike at any moment whether it was smart or not. I forced my feet to stay put. Intruding into this meeting was *not* smart.

"I'll give you the day, my man." Shelton slapped Rafe on the back. "But bring the girl here tonight. I'll make sure she's treated well *and* kept safe," he said, throwing my brother a pointed look.

"No fucking way," Rafe shouted. He lurched forward, and the other guys were on him again.

"Look," Shelton said, holding his arms out at his sides. "It's one fight, and if this feud between the two of you is any fucking indication, it's going to be a helluva match. You both want a shot at each other, and you both want the girl. Sounds like a win-win to me."

I couldn't listen to anymore. As his words sank in,

nausea burned in my throat. I pushed away from the barn and dry-heaved into the brush.

We couldn't go through this again. We might not be trapped in a tunnel this time, but that man in there, imposing his will onto Rafe and me, left my stomach in knots. That fight loomed like a death sentence, especially considering how they were discussing it in a barn, most likely miles from civilization.

This fight would transcend dangerous. It might even be deadly.

And I was the prize.

10. DOUBLE FUCK

RAFE

"Alex stays with me," I said, my voice deathly low and brooking no argument. I would take on every fucking asshole in this barn, leave bloody corpses in my wake before I'd hand over Alex.

Shelton's spine stiffened, and he retreated a negligible inch. Barely noticeable—that sign of concession—but I recognized it for what it was. My rage had festered into an entity, and any fool within a few hundred feet of me could see that. Shelton was no fool.

"Alright," he said. "The girl stays put, but I want her present at the match. Dress her up in something sexy. The crowd will love it."

I bit back a growl, my gaze veering to Zach. For an

insane moment, I almost expected him to give a shit. This was Alex. His sister.

The girl he liked to fuck.

But he couldn't give two fucks whether or not she was dragged into this mess, so long as it benefited him. He didn't wear smug well.

As if Shelton sensed the undercurrent of hostility still zipping back and forth between Zach and me, he instructed his goons to take Zach back to wherever they were keeping the fucker. As the other men herded him from the barn, he ground his teeth at being manhandled.

How do you like it, asshole?

Their exit left Shelton and me alone. I bunched my hands to keep from striking him. "This wasn't what we talked about last night."

"Sure it was," Shelton said in a grating, humoring tone. "You want Zach, and I want a memorable final match worthy of you."

What he wanted was a blood bath that lined his pockets. "You crossed a line by dragging Alex into it. She's been through enough."

"That's just to get *him* onboard. Nothing personal. He thinks he'll win, but I've got my money on you."

"You might be willing to risk Alex, but I'm not."

Shelton folded his arms over his massive chest. "I've got five hundred grand on you in this fight. That's how little De Luca junior concerns me. I never liked his old man, and junior was never as good as you. He knew it. Everyone knew it."

Even so, Zach had caught me off guard once already when he'd shown up on the island. Then a group of thugs had added insult to injury. But that was then, I reminded myself. I'd been fresh out of prison, hadn't trained or fought for a while, and shit had spiraled out of control.

This was now, and for the past six months, I'd dominated inside the cage. I could win this. I knew it in my gut, believed it for one important reason; giving up Alex wasn't an option.

And taking care of Zach was a necessity.

I tapped my foot for several seconds, mulling it over, trying to determine if Shelton could be trusted. "So when I win this, Alex and I are free to jet on out of here, right?"

"I have no intention of burning bridges, Mason. Not good for business, and you've proven to be good for business. It's been years since I had a guy like you fight, so give me a good one before you up and quit on me."

A siren blared in my head. What if I was *too* good for him to let go?

Stop being fucking paranoid, Mason. Not everyone's out to get you.

But even so, the urge to grab Alex and disappear was strong, yet doing so would solve nothing. Zach would still be out there, and I'd be damned if we had to look over our shoulders for the rest of our lives, wondering when he'd catch up to us. If anyone should live in fear, it was Zach. But he didn't operate like a normal human being. Fuck, *I* didn't operate like a normal human being.

"If you fuck me over—"

"Have I ever done wrong by you?"

Not counting the shit he was pulling now? "No, can't say you have." He'd been nothing but good to me. This time, when Shelton stuck his hand out, I pushed past my defenses, logic, common fucking sense, and shook on it. And as I left behind the stench of distrust in that barn, my feet barely out the door, I wanted to turn back. Wanted to change my mind.

Impossible.

If this was the only way to get to Zach without stirring up more trouble, I had to do it. Didn't mean I had to like it though. I returned to the boat, silently screaming obscenities the whole way. My life was a series of clusterfucks.

Would it ever end?

Not even close. I got the second biggest shock of the day once I stepped aboard and entered the cabin. Jax was handcuffed to the damn pole.

He shrugged, throwing me a helpless look. "She found your gun, man, and she looked pissed enough to use it."

Fuck.

I stormed past him and flung the bedroom door open. The dresser was a fucking disaster zone fit for a visit from FEMA. She'd left the drawers open with clothes strewn about, and the drawer where I kept my toys and implements hung precariously off its tracks. Alex was nowhere to be found.

I strode across the room and just as I suspected, she'd taken her purse. A quick swipe underneath the nightstand confirmed the stolen gun.

Double fuck.

As I returned to Jax, I pulled out my cellphone and keys. "How long ago did she leave?"

"Thirty minutes, I guess. Fuck, I don't know. I've been a little tied up here."

"Any idea where she was headed?" I asked, unlocking the cuffs binding him. I pocketed them, figuring they might come in handy.

"She was going after you, dude."

"But she didn't know where I was."

He ran a hand through his hair. "I might've said something about the barn."

"Jeez," I said, shaking my head.

"She was pointing a fucking gun at me. What was I supposed to do?"

"I don't know," I said, attempting to contain my aggravation. "Handle the situation? She wasn't gonna shoot you."

"You didn't see her face. She's not the same scared-shitless girl from six months ago."

"She's upset with me," I muttered, and I couldn't blame her. I'd put her through the wringer—six months ago, last night, even this morning when I'd laid her on the table for breakfast. She had too many questions and no fucking answers.

I dialed her cell and got her voicemail straight away. Either her phone was dead, or she'd shut it off. Or someone had shut it off for her. With a hard swallow, I banished the thought from my mind. Shelton had stowed Zach in shackles somewhere, and he had incentive enough to make sure the fucker stayed there. No one had taken her. Not this time. I refused to believe it, so that meant she'd gone off on her own.

But why?

Rubbing his wrists, Jax leaned against the bench, and I sank onto the sofa across from him.

"Shelton wants me to fight Zach, with Alex as the prize. If she followed me to the barn…" I cursed under my breath. "She might've overheard something she shouldn't have."

"Or she's scared out of her mind after pulling a fucking gun on me." Jax's face hardened. "She should be scared. You need to get that shit under control pronto."

He might be right, but I couldn't drive away the

anxiety in my stomach. If she'd overheard us, then she'd seen Zach. Maybe she'd removed herself from the situation so she couldn't be used as a bargaining chip. Seemed like something she'd do.

But had she taken off because she was worried about my part in this upcoming fight, or because she was afraid for her brother? Did she sense how badly I wanted to rip into him? Maybe she'd caught a whiff of the metaphorical blood on my hands, and the realization that she was in love with a monster had sent her packing— had sent her careening over the cliff, a thread away from another mental meltdown.

"Fuck. I've gotta find her."

11. REBELLIOUS

ALEX

I'd never hitchhiked in my life. Luckily for me, the woman who picked me up wasn't a psychopath. Maybe fate had decided I'd had enough run-ins with the dark and sinister type. Ironically, hitching a ride with a stranger was probably about as safe as merely breathing.

She pulled alongside the curb in downtown Portland and wished me luck.

"Thanks for letting me tag along," I said, pushing the passenger door open.

The frigid air whipped my messy hair into my face. I swiped the locks from my eyes, standing on the sidewalk as I watched my Good Samaritan wheel away in her SUV. I was surprised she'd let me into her pristine ride, considering how my sneakers were caked in mud from hiking through the soggy fields surrounding the barn. I must have spent forty-five minutes walking before I found the highway, and another half hour waiting until someone picked me up. The whole time, I'd agonized over Rafe finding me…and agonized over whether or not I wanted him to.

Shivering in my hoodie that was barely thick enough to ward off a breeze, let alone temperatures this low, I dug my phone out and stared at the blank screen. I'd shut the thing off during my trek through the fields, afraid that Rafe would call, and I'd lose my nerve to flee.

Even now, I was scared to turn it back on—not that I had anyone I could call to pick me up. I could call Evelyn, but I hadn't spoken to her since the day Zach's phone call had ruined my lunch with her. Besides, dragging anyone into this situation was selfish. My therapist was the only person I felt comfortable enough to talk to. Sandra would offer an unbiased ear—unbiased except for where the law was concerned. If I unloaded everything on her, she'd insist on contacting the police, and sure, they'd arrest my brother. But what about Rafe? He was participating in illegal fighting. I wouldn't be the reason he went back to jail. Never again.

But something needed to change because I couldn't go on like this anymore. I was lost, a wanderer inside my life, herded along by the will of others, and it needed to stop.

I spotted a coffee shop less than a block away, and my stomach grumbled, reminding me that I hadn't eaten yet. As I hurried down the sidewalk, that cafe called to me with the warmth it offered. I entered, letting out a relieved sigh, and rubbed my hands together while I waited in line to order a cappuccino and something sinful to nibble on.

The young guy behind the counter was too swamped with customers to pay extra attention to me, which suited me fine. Settling at a small table in the corner away from other people, I bit into a pastry, sipped from my steaming cappuccino, and wished for the power of invisibility. I needed my car so I could get the hell out of Dodge.

Because thinking with a clear head was impossible around Rafe. He hypnotized me with his presence, with the way he played my body as if I were his personal instrument. At that moment, surrounded by normal people enjoying their Sunday in a coffee shop, escaping the chill of winter, I realized how badly I was reeling.

My cell taunted me from the table, its mere presence screaming how I couldn't avoid Rafe forever. Picking up the phone, I powered it up, and just as I feared, several missed call notifications blared at me from the screen. A shrill ring made me jump, and I slid the green bar to the right, brought the phone to my ear with trembling fingers, and whispered a hello.

"Where the fuck are you?" Rafe's frantic voice issued a sharp pang through my temple.

Shit, he was mad.

"Somewhere safe."

"You think you're safer on your own than with me?"

I gazed around the shop, but no one was paying me any attention. Just in case, I kept my voice low. "I won't be the prize in a fight. I'm not a piece of meat."

"What you are is mine, and you're gonna tell me where you are."

I gritted my teeth. "I'll kill myself before I let Zach get his hands on me again. And next time, I won't botch up the job."

A growl filtered through the phone. "I'll spank your ass black and blue if you ever talk like that again."

As if he were standing over me, threatening to punish me in person, my muscles tightened.

He let out a breath, and his furious tone evened out. "Where are you? I'll come pick you up."

"N-no."

"Sweetheart," he warned.

"Not until you call off this fight with Zach."

An aggravated sigh traveled through the line. "I can't do that."

"Please, Rafe," I begged, blinking, horrified that I was nearly crying in public. "Do it for me."

"I *am* doing this for you!" he shouted. I winced,

holding the phone away from my ear until the screeching stopped. "Tell me where you are right now, or I swear to God—"

I pressed the button to end the call, powered off the phone, and gazed at my shaking hand. I didn't know how long I sat there, zoning out, the quiet chatter lulling me into a sense of peace. Except reality was waiting beyond the door of this temporary haven, and I didn't know what to do.

Run, or go back to him?

The idea of running, of never seeing him again, broke my heart, but I couldn't go back while things were the way they were. I suspected he'd taken me because Zach posed a threat. He loved me enough to protect me, but after witnessing his nightmare while pinned under the lethal strength of his hands, after overhearing his phone call this morning, I realized, even if he didn't, that he still blamed me too.

I stood on quaking legs and made my way to the exit, avoiding eye contact with people. Could they tell how rattled I was by looking at me? Not even the blistering cold could penetrate the dread coiling around my body.

I'd just hung up on him.

What the hell was I thinking? But I wasn't thinking, and that was the problem. I hopped on a city bus, my mind as frozen as the weather, and after a couple hours and two transfers, I reached my neighborhood as night descended. This wasn't how I thought I'd spend my Sunday. Seemed like Rafe had taken me days ago, yet a mere 24 hours had passed since I found him lurking in the shadows just inside my foyer.

As I approached my house on foot, a Ford pickup caught my eye, parked a few houses down by the curb. Instantly, I knew it belonged to Rafe. I'd never seen it on my street, and his presence beyond my door hit me in waves, as if I felt him in there, waiting for me, his anger palpable.

My car sat untouched in the driveway, and I had my keys in my purse. I could climb in and drive away. But then what? Where would I go?

I had nowhere to go. I only had him. I only *wanted* him.

But did he want me because the thought of being apart made him ill, or was the threat of Zach the reason Rafe had come back into my life after all these months? I couldn't turn away without knowing, regardless of how much the sane part of me wanted to. Preparing myself for the ultimate showdown, I climbed the icy steps and went inside.

12. TICK TOCK

RAFE

I paced Alex's small kitchen and glared at my cell for the hundredth time. No lie. Since she'd hung up on me, my eyes could have burned a hole through that frustratingly silent phone. I'd called her back too many times to keep track of, and each time I heard her voicemail, I wanted to put my fist through a wall.

She was fucking lucky I hadn't turned her house upside down. Too much energy flushed my system, so I paced. I waited. I raided her damn fridge, downing two stray beers I suspected Jax had left during one of his check-in visits.

And I imagined all kinds of crazy shit.

Was she with someone else? Some other guy I'd have

to kill because the thought of Alex with anyone else made me see red. Or maybe she'd hopped on a bus or train, headed for parts unknown. What was she *thinking*? I thought she'd make her way back since she lived here… except that wasn't quite right either. Her home was with me, and mine was with her, wherever we ended up.

But her fucking car was still parked in the driveway. If she were on the run, surely she'd need her damn car.

Tick tock, tick tock, but no Alex. *Where* was she? When I did get my hands on her…

She had no idea how much this was tearing me up, not knowing where she was, not knowing if she was safe or on the verge of a breakdown. My imagination galloped ahead, and I envisioned her in a bathtub full of blood with deep gashes in her wrists. I didn't think she was suicidal, but I couldn't wipe history from my overactive mind. I should have never left her six months ago.

The knob on the front door turned, and I tried to calm the sudden flow of adrenaline rushing my veins. I shut off the light over the stove. It was the only light I'd switched on after gaining entrance to her house with the key Jax had supplied me with months ago. The one she'd never known about.

I heard the door open and close, then the latch of a deadbolt. Moving into the foyer with light steps, I aimed to take her by surprise, but her words stopped me cold.

"I know you're here, so there's no need to sneak up

on me." She flipped on the light by the door, and her eyes met mine. She'd known I was waiting, yet she'd come inside anyway.

I let out a breath. "You're not fucking running from me," I said, keeping my voice even. But I must have hit a nerve.

"*You're* the one good at running," she snapped. "Zach is the only reason you came back, isn't he?" Tears welled in her eyes, and for once, I didn't want to pounce on them.

I was guilty. Zach's escape had been the precipitous event that sent me careening toward her, but it wasn't the *only* reason, and the fact that she didn't know that pissed me off.

It also made me kick myself.

She wiped under her jade eyes, and her burning gaze flagellated me with hurt and indignant anger.

"I want you to go," she whispered. "Do what you need to do in that stupid barn."

"I'm not leaving you here—"

"Just go away!" she screamed, hurtling her purse at me. I ducked, and the thing hit the wall behind my head. A bang went off, and we both jumped. I let the expletives fly then gaped at the remains of her purse.

"The fuck, Alex?"

"Oh my God...the gun..." she sobbed, covering her face with shaking hands. She whirled and reached for the doorknob as if she couldn't believe what she'd nearly done and needed to run from it.

I sprang forward and pulled her against me, shackling her in the cage of my arms. She shook with unrestrained sobs.

"I'm s-sorry," she said with a hiccup. "I didn't mean it."

"I know you didn't. Stop fighting me."

"Just let me go."

I dropped my arms and slid around her, inserting myself between her and escape. She tried to maneuver past me, but I blocked her, stepping to the right when she did, then to the left. She came to a halt, her shoulders slumping in defeat.

"This is all…you and me…" She waved a hand between us, her words broken by the pain constricting her voice. "This is all just to keep me safe, right? I'm nothing but an obligation."

Taking her by the shoulders, I turned around and backed her against the door. Fuck. Now I wanted the tears. Even her anger because it didn't sear me the way her desolation did. "Baby, your douchebag brother only gave me an excuse to do the wrong thing here."

Tears slid down her face, and her breaths came fast and shallow. "You left a hole in my heart. It took me six months, but…" Avoiding my eyes, she gulped. "I don't need you anymore."

"Well I need you!" I shook her shoulders, trying to banish the apathy from her bones. She was a fucking liar, cold, shut down with insurmountable walls in place. But why? Had the sight of Zach sent her into this state, or was it my fault? "I need you so fucking much. Don't make me beg."

The current between us sizzled, shifted, and she pulled my mouth down on hers, teeth tugging on my lip. She was a demanding little vixen in that kiss, and I was a goner. Her fingers sifted through my hair, clutched and pulled.

"Trust me," I murmured against her lips. "I took you because I wanted to." Another slow slide of our tongues stole my sanity. "Making you bend is all I think about," I rasped between more kisses. "The thought of never sinking inside you again drives me insane."

She drew back and peered at me with a splotchy face, studying me like I was a fucking enigma. "How much trouble am I in?" A hint of fear laced those words. She was too smart not to realize how screwed she was.

"A lot."

"What do you want from me?" she nearly shrieked. She'd given so much of herself already, but it would never be enough. I'd always want more. I sensed she was beginning to understand the consequences of being with someone like me, and it scared her.

My memory loss had shown her a gentler side, and

even though that guy wasn't completely dead and gone, he wasn't in the driver seat now. But she wanted him. She'd pleaded for the harsh reality of the guy who'd taken want he wanted from her, but underneath it all, she yearned for normalcy.

Kindness.

Gentleness with a little kink.

She didn't want to give up control, or if she did, she struggled with it.

"I want you safe," I bit out, gripping her chin. "I want you fucking crying." To emphasize my words, I tightened my grip on her jaw. "Most of all, I want you naked and tied down on my boat, helpless." I angled my head, waiting for some sort of reaction. "I want you begging for the pain to stop."

"No," she said in a breathless whisper though that single word packed a punch. She nibbled on her lip, her gaze pensive…aroused. Fuck, my dick wanted out to play. How did she do this to me?

"Are you really telling me no?"

"Yes." The tip of her tongue darted along the seam of her stubborn mouth. "I have a condition."

"What would that be?"

"Tell me the truth. If Zach hadn't gotten away, would you have come for me?" Her expression screamed what she didn't say. She wanted to know if I could be so heartless as to leave her forever thinking I was dead. I was that heartless, but only because I did want to protect her.

From me.

This fucker right here who was close to shoving her over the arm of her couch and ramming his cock in her ass, simply because taking her that way pushed her beyond her limits.

And he wouldn't ask for permission.

This guy was a doer, the type of man that didn't rehash every moment of his history with her and let it dictate his next move. This guy was *me*.

The new and improved me with nasty blood-filled memories and all.

"Yes," I said. "I would have, eventually, because nothing on this fucking Earth can save you from me."

13. EMPTY GOLD

ALEX

Rafe intoxicated me with his high-octane sex appeal. I wasn't sure he realized just how potent he was. My head drowned in lust's deep end, and my fear and anger and sadness—none of it combatted the fact that had I been wearing panties, I would have drenched them by now. As it was, my need for him dripped down the inside of my thighs, no doubt soaking through my jeans.

"I don't want to be saved. I want to be fucked." I stared him down, daring him to deny me this time. He wouldn't—not with the way his green eyes sparked, or the unconscious way he pulled his lower lip, still damp from my kiss, between desperate teeth.

He rested his forehead against mine and groaned.

"You tempt me, my little slut."

I slid my hand past his drawstring waistband, glad he hadn't changed into pants with annoying buttons and zippers, and wrapped my fingers around his hard cock. "Look who's talking," I said, swirling my thumb over the silky head.

"Shit, baby." And that was the last thing he said for a while. Our mouths clashed in a warring feud. We couldn't get enough of each other. I slid my palms under his shirt, up his chest, dragging the soft cotton along for the ride. He pulled back long enough to yank it from his body, and the shirt flew behind him somewhere, lost in the shadows of my living room.

We slowly made our way in that direction, losing more clothing on the way. After I shed my jeans, he hoisted me in his embrace, hands firm on my hips. I wrapped my legs around him, and he twirled until we fell onto the couch with me on top. I straddled him, my hair falling all around us, and drove onto his cock in a downward thrust.

With a grunt, he lifted me, sucked my nipple into his mouth and bit down hard, then jerked me to his lap again. "Harder, babe," he demanded, breathless.

I slammed onto him and cried out, fingers curling into the cushions on the back of the couch. Something animalistic took over. He grabbed my nape and brought me closer, sucked on my throat, scraped his teeth across the tender flesh there. Letting go of the sofa, I clutched his hair and tugged, making him growl in pain.

He rose, bringing me with him, and we stumbled down the hall, slamming into one side then the other, his cock still nestled inside me, our lips and hands everywhere.

"We're so fucked," he said, nibbling my ear.

"Fucked is feeling damn spectacular right now."

His laughter rumbled down the side of my neck. "Shit, babe, I'm gonna come inside you. I don't think I can stop."

Why would he want to? "Don't stop," I pleaded. I never wanted this to end. We stumbled deeper into the hall, and I pushed a door open. "The bed," was all I managed to say. He carried me through the blackness, staggering the whole way, and we plummeted to the mattress. Hurtled toward abandon.

Pushing my leg up, he dangled it over his shoulder before slamming so deep, it hurt in the best way imaginable. Teeth nipped at skin. Nails scratched the path of insanity. Fingers clutched with possession. Groans rent the air. He was just as vocal, which was the biggest turn on of all.

"My little slut," he said, moaning into the crook of my shoulder with each thrust of his cock. "You own me, baby. You fucking have me wrapped."

We had each other wrapped, or I wouldn't have entered my house knowing he was waiting. I would have gotten in my car and fled. Would have put as much distance as possible between us because I'd known the instant I'd pulled that gun on Jax, there'd be hell to pay.

I hadn't wanted to face it. I still didn't want to. But life without him was incomprehensible. I'd pay, and dearly, but for now I'd take every second of him fucking me like he'd never fuck me again.

"Let's just freeze this moment, Rafe. Stay inside me forever."

He shoved my hands over my head, his fingers a tight band around my wrists, and stilled inside me. "We're both gonna come hard, then I'm taking your ass home to be punished. You're not getting out of it."

"What are you gonna do? Tell me." That way, I could prepare.

"And ruin the fun? Don't think so." He jutted his hips forward, and we settled into a lazy, pussy-drenching tempo.

"Oh...ohhhh...fuuuuck."

"You're so wet," he said with a gruff whisper.

"You do this to me." It was building...something that scared and excited me because I sensed the drop from that euphoric cloud would be devastating. "I need to touch you." I fisted my hands, wishing I could escape the circle of his grip.

In answer, he entwined our fingers. "You are touching me. You touch me just by loving me." He kissed me long and deep, his tongue exploring every part of my mouth as his cock slid in and out at a slow, maddening pace.

"Marry me," he gasped, severing our mouths. He stilled inside me again, and I was sure my eyes bulged. Huge. Full of disbelief.

"Wh-what?"

"You heard me."

"But—"

"You're not allowed to tell me no." His lips brushed over mine, twitching at the corners.

I was at a loss for words, but telling him no had never been an option anyway. Me married to Rafe Mason. I stuttered a yes. At least I think I did. He was moving again in that slow way he was such a fucking expert at.

And I was coming...again.

A groan rumbled from his chest as I liquefied around his cock. "Right now. Marry me."

"Now? Rafe...*Oh God!*" My spine bowed, and my neck veered back as I held onto his hands. Fuuuuck. I thought I was done, but he still had me going, still kept the unhurried rhythm that hit my sweet spot just right.

"Baby, *'Oh God'* isn't the vow I'm looking for."

I cried out his name again. "I-I can't...think...when you're fucking me like this..."

"I can stop fucking you like this."

I whimpered. "Don't you dare."

"Marry me now, while I'm deep inside of you."

I squeezed his fingers. "I promise to love you—" I gasped, groaned, cursed to the heavens. All of the above. I was lost.

"Keep going," he said.

"I promise to give you my tears." A drop slid down my cheek, and he licked it up with a sigh. "Promise to give you my body, my soul," my voice cracked. "Promise to give you my pain. Always."

"That's what I wanna hear." He gathered my wrists in one hand and gripped my throat with the other. "I promise to cherish you." His voice was laden with the oath of so much more. "I'll spend forever earning your trust." His fingers tightened, pressing against the staccato *thump-thump-thump* of my heartbeat pulsing in my neck, and my head started swimming. "I'll fucking protect you with my life."

"Rafe?" I rasped.

"What is it, baby?"

"I'm scared." I thought I could handle him choking me, but the terror of him taking my air in his sleep held me captive. Something in him had changed—recovering his memories and spending six months apart had changed him. Changed us both.

"What are you scared of?"

"I don't know."

"Close your eyes."

I did so, and he pounded into me with rough thrusts,

increasing the pace, his breathing labored as he neared climax. "Feel me inside you? I'll never hurt you. Do you trust me?"

"Y-yes." I wanted to trust him.

"You're mine. I never harm what's mine." The pressure on my throat intensified, and my eyes flew open. I couldn't help it—I panicked. Screeching like a tortured animal, I tried wrenching my hands from his large fist, but he wouldn't let go—of my wrists or my neck.

I flailed under the weight of him, my efforts useless, and eventually gave in to the inevitable, reminding myself that this was what I'd pleaded for months ago.

To be at his mercy. For him to take control.

To hurt me.

Be careful what you wish for.

He'd owned the darkness inside him, and nothing I did or said would stop him. He choked the breath from me without reservation, and the last thing I remembered was his whispered vow that he'd never let me go.

14. ADDICTION

RAFE

I clung to the high, to the memory of her struggle as I squeezed the breath from her. The last time I remembered coming that fucking hard was…

Back on the island, the first time I'd fucked her. The first time I'd *choked* her.

Oh hell.

This could become an addiction. Forget heroin or cocaine or even fucking ecstasy. All I needed was Alex's throat trapped in the vise of my fingers while her deviant cunt gloved my cock.

A weak beam of moonlight filtered through her curtains, bathing her pale, sweat-doused skin. I traced the letters of my name and felt her belly rumble underneath my touch. Lifting my head, I took in her glazed-over expression, her limp arms above her head. She looked thoroughly fucked and much too satisfied.

"You back down from that cloud yet?"

A small smile teased the corners of her mouth. "No."

Choking her had scared the fuck out of her, but when she'd returned to consciousness, my cock had sent her even higher. My fucking cock might've knocked her up too. I had more self-control than this…as least I thought I did.

Her stomach groaned again.

"What did you eat today?" I asked.

"Um…not much."

Not surprising, knowing what I knew about her eating habits. I pushed onto my elbows and slid from the mattress. "Be right back."

"Where're you going?" she asked, her lazy gaze following me across the room toward the door we'd left wide open in our haste to fuck on her bed.

"To find food."

"Okay," she mumbled, and I think she would have agreed even if I'd said I was going to talk to aliens.

I searched the living room for my discarded clothes and pulled on my sweats before entering the kitchen. I turned on the stove light and listened for a few seconds to make sure she hadn't followed. I didn't need her overhearing the phone call I was about to make, so I turned on the stove fan as well. Opening the fridge, I eyed the meager contents as I dialed Jax. He answered almost immediately.

"You find her?"

"Yeah." I also fucked her brains out. Shit. "How's the birth control situation coming?"

"You fucked her." Not a question, but a statement. "I figured it was gonna happen, so I picked up a magic *everything's-all-right* pill with the prescription."

I let out a breath. "I owe you."

"Let's not get into who owes who, okay? Just get her ass back here because I want to be there when you punish her. She cocked that fucking gun at me, man."

I pulled some questionable looking lunch meat from the second shelf, followed by cheese and Mayo." The bread on the counter was a bit dry, but it hadn't molded over yet, so I figured it was edible. Cradling the phone between my shoulder and ear, I began putting together two sandwiches. "I'll let you punish her yourself if you do something else for me."

He whistled. "Didn't see that one coming."

My eyes veered to the darkened hall. "She's earned it. She was reckless. Not only did she threaten you, but she put herself in danger." Not to mention she could have fucking killed *me* when that gun went off. She was too damn smart to pull shit like that.

"I'm all ears. Whaddya have in mind?"

As I finished making the food, I told Jax my plans and what I needed him to do. "It's late, so we're gonna crash here, but we'll be back tomorrow. I'll give you a heads up when I'm on my way." Ending the call, I pocketed my cell and grabbed both plates. I found her dozing, sprawled in the middle of the bed like she owned it…which I guess she did.

I switched on the light, and her eyes fluttered open. With a yawn, she scooted over as I approached.

"I'm sorry for fucking you like that," I said, my weight depressing the mattress. I handed her a plate, but she set it beside her on the bed and looked at me in confusion.

"How can you say that to me?" Or maybe hurt was etched into her face instead. Hard to tell, but she pulled the sheet to her chest, instantly erecting walls between us. "Tonight was—"

"Fucking amazing," I whispered, leaning forward and stealing her mouth for a few seconds. "That's not what I meant. I'm not sorry for fucking you. I'm sorry for doing it without a condom."

Her eyes widened as if she only now realized the colossal mistake we'd made. "Oh God."

"Hey," I said, taking her chin in my hand. "I'm taking care of it. I *never* want to put us in this position again."

She bit her lip, and I couldn't stop from taking her mouth, one hand cradling her head as I plunged deep. Fucking hell, *amazing* didn't even do it justice, and all I

118

could think about was doing it again. And again. We'd never leave this bed.

Before we got carried away—again—I broke away and nudged her plate. "Eat. I know you're hungry."

She picked up the sandwich and bit into it, chewed slowly, but her gaze held a question.

"Something on your mind?"

"When are you taking me back to the boat?"

I settled beside her and started in on my own dry, tasteless dinner. "It's late. We'll stay here tonight." And just because I couldn't resist messing with her head, I added, "You better get some sleep, sweetheart. You're gonna need your strength for tomorrow, trust me."

15. BURN

ALEX

After a breakfast of cereal and two overripe bananas the next morning, Rafe told me to get cleaned up. "Wear a skirt, no panties." His kiss fractured clear thought, and my core flooded with desire. I stared at him like a dumbass as he left and closed the door behind him.

I used the bathroom first, taking a hot shower and tempting myself with the idea of sliding my fingers between my legs. Last night replayed in my mind like a dirty fantasy, but every moment had been real. Before I gave in to temptation, I shut off the water and stepped out with steam rising off my skin.

Last thing I wanted was to provoke him, so I followed his orders and dressed in a longer skirt to protect my legs from the cold. I was feeling good, the confrontation of yesterday diminished by our free-fall into bed last night. Still riding that wave, I was *not* prepared for the sight that greeted me in the living room. He sat on the couch dangling the same type of cuffs I'd used on Jax yesterday. Maybe even the same set.

I skidded to a stop, alarmed. "What do you think you're doing?"

"You stole my gun and left the boat. You could've killed me when it went off in your tantrum." He rose slowly and came toward me, cuffs gripped in his hands. "I'm not letting that slide."

"What are you gonna do?"

"Punish your ass when we get back. What else do you think I'm gonna do?"

Guess the honeymoon was over. "This is ridiculous." I retreated another step, heading toward the other end of the sofa. "What if I don't wanna go back?"

His mouth veered up in a lopsided, know-it-all-smirk. "You didn't have permission to leave the boat, and you sure as fuck didn't have my okay to take my gun and go all badass chick on Jax with it." He gestured toward my hands. "Consequences, sweetheart. Turn the fuck around."

"No way!" I zipped to the other side of the couch.

"Get over here *now*."

Oh, he was pissed. The thin line of his lips captivated

me, the gravelly timbre of his voice. Something primal in me responded, as it always did when he took that tone. Shit, I was wet already, and he hadn't laid a finger on me.

"You want me over there?" I taunted, pointing to where he stood, primed to move in an instant.

"Stupid question, babe." He held up the cuffs and dangled them with a smug grin.

I stepped right, but so did he. "What do I get in return?"

"A sore ass?"

I gnawed on my lip to hide a moan, but I figured he saw right through me. This felt a bit like a game; one we both knew the plays to. I knew he was going to punish me, and he knew I wasn't putting up a real fight.

But I did want something.

"Fine, I'll give you my hands if you promise me something."

"I don't negotiate, sweetheart. You're gonna give me your hands anyway."

"Please," I begged, my fingers slowly undoing the first two buttons of my top. I slipped a hand inside and fondled my left breast.

"You're fucking pushing it, Alex." He sauntered closer, his fingers flexing around the metal shackles. He wanted my wrists locked in them badly—I could tell by the twitch in his jaw and the heat in his eyes. "What do you want?"

"Answers," I said.

He tilted his head. "Answers?"

"Yeah." I withdrew my hand from my shirt and gestured between us. "You know, where you actually *talk* to me?"

He rounded the sofa, careful to keep his steps light and easy, preying on me as if I were a skittish animal.

"I'll give you two questions after you're done taking your punishment."

"Two questions?" I raised an indignant brow. "Is that all my surrender is worth to you?"

"*Three questions*," he bit out through clenched teeth.

"Four." I retreated a couple of inches.

"Three. That's my final offer."

There was no offer. If I said yes, if I said no…he'd still have my hands in those cuffs and my ass in his truck headed back to the boat. I could fight him. I could run.

But I didn't want to. Running from Rafe Mason seemed counter-intuitive.

The heavy weight of reality pressed on my chest, leaving no space for light-hearted fun. Not when my insanity held me captive. Rafe would let me go if I put up a good enough fight. I knew he would. For all the black desires and demons he battled, his conscience ruled the better part of him, or he wouldn't have left me six months ago.

My eyes burned with helplessness, and I turned my

face away, hating how he witnessed my weakness. His soft footfalls grew closer, and warm fingertips slid along my arms, over my hideous scars. With no effort at all, he turned me and locked my wrists in place at the small of my back. Whirling me around again, he tried to get my attention, but I refused to look at him. The brush of his fingers on my chin demanded I meet his gaze.

"Are you scared of the water? Do you need me to drug you?"

It wasn't a threat. He was asking out of genuine concern, and in some fucked-up way, that only made me love him more. I was a prisoner of my traitorous heart. The damn bloody organ didn't know what was good for me. "I'll manage."

"Okay, let's get this over with." He grabbed me by the shoulder and ushered me into the morning chill.

"Three questions," I reminded him as he locked the front door behind us. We descended the steps, careful not to slip on ice, and made our way to his red truck. I wondered what my neighbors would think if they peeked between their curtains and saw Rafe herding me down the street with my hands cuffed at my back. But my street was quiet with most of the driveways empty and the drapes closed. Typical for a Monday morning.

He opened the passenger side, helped me slide onto the seat, and strapped me in the confines of the safety belt. I wasn't sure why he'd felt the need to cuff my hands at all—it wasn't like I was going to fight him.

Not really.

He had to know that.

"Three questions," he said, brushing a stray curl from my eyes. "Whatever you want to know, I'll tell you the truth, I promise."

But my pain would come first, and considering Jax's vow that he'd be present when Rafe dished out punishment, probably my degradation as well. I blinked several times but ultimately let the tears fall. I didn't want to piss him off more by breaking yet another rule.

"Jax is going to be there for this, isn't he?"

He caught a teardrop on his thumb and dipped it between his lips. "You threatened to shoot him," was all he said before shutting the door.

Answer enough. He started the ignition, and I watched with growing dread as my house faded in the distance. At some point, I dozed off, my head lopsided on my neck and resting against the cool glass. By the time he silenced the engine, my shoulders were on fire from being restrained.

He helped me from the rig and circled behind me. "Close your eyes," he said, shuttering my vision with his hands. Slowly, he pushed us forward, and the instant we stepped onto the dock and it swayed, my stomach took a nosedive.

"Rafe!"

"I've got you," he said, tightening his hold. "Almost there." We shuffled a few more feet, our shoes gliding over the slick dock. With a steady hand, he helped me onto the boat. The whole time, I kept my eyes sealed shut. We descended the stairs, and only then did I open them to find Jax waiting in the galley with his arms crossed.

Rafe gestured for me to sit down, and when Jax saw my cuffed hands, he grinned. At least he had the grace not to say anything about it.

He passed Rafe a small bag. "Instructions are in there."

"I won't even ask how you got your hands on this."

"I know people. Contraceptives are easy as fuck to get when you've got contacts in the sex trade."

"Yeah, I don't need the reminder of your underground contacts, but thanks."

"No problem."

"Everything ready?"

"You bet it is." Jax flexed his hands, eyes raking over me, and not in a lascivious way, but in an *I'm gonna make you pay* way.

"Rafe, what are you gonna—"

He placed two fingers over my lips. "You don't talk. You follow orders. If you need to cry or scream, I'm fine with that. But not a word until I say so." He removed his fingers and leaned down, close enough that his breath fanned over my trembling lips. "When we're done, I'll give you your three questions."

I couldn't help but wonder if he was pissed because I'd disobeyed him, or because I'd talked him into giving me the fucking truth after he finished taking his pleasure from my pain and humiliation. I wanted to ask, wanted to beg him to tell me what they planned to do, but he wasn't messing around now. He meant every word. Somehow, I knew he was going to hurt me beyond anything I'd ever experienced. This punishment would transcend all others.

I bit my lip to keep from opening my damn mouth. He was being gentle with me, but an undercurrent of anger flowed into the room, coming off him and Jax.

I'd made a colossal mistake by running.

"Go into the bedroom and bend over the end of the bed. Don't move, no matter how much time passes."

Swallowing hard with a loud gulp, I rose and dragged my reluctant feet into the bedroom. I bent over the mattress and winced from the deep ache in my shoulders. And I waited.

Eventually, they made their presence known. Rafe set the bag Jax had given him on the dresser, then he moved behind me and kicked my feet apart. He released my hands from the metal cuffs and bound them together with rope. Lifting my arms behind me, he tethered my wrists to the anchor in the ceiling. I let out a screech of pain through gritted teeth.

Jax removed my shoes and tied down my ankles to the rings in the floor. I couldn't close my legs. I couldn't lift my shoulders off the bed because doing so hurt too much. They had me spread and helpless. Just like they wanted me. My pulse skittered at my throat, increasing until it blasted my chest with pain.

No way out.

"You're fucking stubborn and reckless," Rafe said, lifting my skirt, trailing his hands up my exposed bare bottom. He tucked the material around my hips and under my belly. I shivered as he gripped my ass with unforgiving fingers. "I won't stand for it." He returned to the dresser and picked up a bowl. "What if Zach had been waiting?"

A rhetorical question since I wasn't allowed to speak, but hell if I didn't want to ask what was in that bowl.

"You put yourself at risk by leaving Jax's protection. You put all of us at risk by taking my gun. Now you're gonna pay for it." Water sloshed, and a few seconds later, something hard and cold pressed against my rectum. He hadn't lubed me first. Oh God. The pressure increased, and I clenched my teeth to keep from opening my mouth.

The smooth object passed the point of burning, giving me a reprieve, and I breathed through my nose in intense relief. Soft footsteps retreated, and I sensed him watching me, his gaze burning a wave of heat over my backside. If he ran his finger up my slit, he'd find it embarrassingly wet. Shit, I might be dripping all over the floor, for all I knew, since my thighs had been forced wide open.

Whatever he'd inserted grew warm, giving me a feeling of fullness that hurt and aroused. But then the sensation amped hotter…hotter still.

It fucking scorched.

"Take it out!" I screamed, clenching my bottom, but that only made the burn intolerable.

Rafe removed his belt from a drawer, looped it in a fist…then he fucking offered it to Jax. "Unless you'd rather use your hand. Either is fine with me."

"No! Please, Rafe—" My voice cut out on a sob.

"I'll use my hand," Jax said.

Rafe leaned against the dresser, arms crossed, right in my direct line of view. "He's gonna spank you ten times, babe, and if you say another fucking word, I'll make it double."

Oh god, my rectum blazed—was the most intense pain I'd experienced in my life. The sting of Jax's hand wouldn't compare. At the thought of Jax touching me, shame as hot and as swift flushed my skin. My traitorous pussy throbbed in tandem with the agony. I couldn't control my body, and I wanted to now, more than ever.

Pain is pleasure.

My body was whacked.

"What'd you put in there?" I demanded, despite

Rafe's gag order.

Rafe closed the distance, bent over, and swept his tongue over my cheek. "Ginger," he said, voice raw with arousal. "If you can't be quiet and take your punishment, I *will* gag you." When he returned to his spot in front of the dresser, the bulge in his pants had grown even bigger.

"Give her twenty, whenever you're ready," he told Jax with a wave of his hand.

I wasn't ready.

Jax brought his hand down, and I bit on my lip hard until I tasted blood, but I still couldn't keep from clenching the muscles in my ass.

"Ahhh!" The more I cried out, the harder Jax spanked me.

And the wetter I became.

Rafe inched the waistband of his sweats lower, taking his time, his fingers moving in slow motion...at least, they seemed to. I became obsessed with that torturous slide of material, my concentration stuck on what lay beyond. The strikes receded in my mind. My world narrowed to Rafe's cock as he whipped it out and pumped a determined fist up and down his smooth shaft.

"Eyes up here."

I raised my gaze to his. Holy shit. His eyes were the greenest of green, turned deep from arousal. Suddenly, I didn't care that I was sprawled out for Jax to beat. Suddenly...the retribution he took from my skin made

130

sense. I'd pointed a gun at him, left him handcuffed, and had taken off like a brat. Didn't matter how fucked up my logic was. If watching another man punish me made Rafe look at me like *that*, then it was worth it.

The burn in my ass subsided during the last couple of minutes though my skin tingled from where Jax's palm landed over and over again. Eventually, the swats ceased, and Rafe carefully removed the ginger. I let out a noisy sigh of relief.

It was over. Except...

Was Rafe *snickering*?

"You'd better brace yourself." Footsteps sounded, water sloshed *again*...

Oh no.

He inched another piece into my tender hole, and I started whimpering as I realized what I was in for. I questioned my earlier assessment as I waited for the burn to once again ignite. It wasn't over at all—Rafe was just warming up.

16. VOYEUR

RAFE

I'd seen Alex in so many positions, so many situations. Some perversely fucked up—the kind that brought swift shame because my cock had gotten hard when it shouldn't have…such as in that tunnel when Cleft forced her mouth on me.

But this…

Seeing her bound, her body covered in sweat and unable to squirm without inducing an intense scorch in her ass, this was my twisted version of heaven. I never thought I'd get so worked up over examining the marks left on her ass by another man.

I clenched the belt, adrenaline coursing through my veins, and ached to bring the strap down on that canvas of beautiful, painful pink.

"Apologize to Jax for pulling my gun on him." She sniffled, attempting to hold back her sobs. "Go on, Alex. I give you permission to speak now."

"Fuck you."

I blasted the leather across her ass. "Not what I had in mind, sweetheart."

"Take it out! You've had your fun."

"No. *Jax* had his fun. Now it's my turn, but you're gonna tell him sorry first."

"I'm sorry," she bit out, her tone suggesting she was anything but. I whipped her thighs this time. She jumped, then screamed from the amped up severity.

"Fucking…Rafe!" She flexed her hands, stiffened her legs, but God help her—she didn't dare clench her ass. "I'm sorry!"

"Sorry for what?" I trailed the strap over her reddened cheeks, enjoying how her legs quivered.

"For taking your gun."

"And?"

"For pulling it on Jax. I won't do it again."

I dropped the belt on the bed, and when I laid my palms on her warm bottom, she jumped again, letting out a hiss of pain between gritted teeth. But when I slipped a finger into her cunt, I found it soaked. Her body mystified me, entranced me, owned me right to the tip of my cock.

"You don't have to stick around for this," I told Jax, sensing him lingering from the corner of my eye.

He shifted, gaining my attention, and leaned against the wall with his shoulders slumped. "Mind if I watch?"

I grasped my belt once more and shuffled back a few steps. "Go ahead." But would *he* mind? Would watching me with Alex be too much for him? I didn't want to ask, and I didn't want to make things worse by implying he leave either.

"You're getting twenty more," I told Alex. "And you're gonna count them." Jax had gone easy on her. I wouldn't, not after the hell she'd put me through yesterday. He'd left her ass a beautiful shade, using nothing more than the angry palm of his hand. But I planned to leave welts—the kind of reminder that she was *mine*. As I brought down that belt for real this time, my bicep bulging in delivering a brutal *crack*, I probably hated myself more than she did, because her cry of agony rushed through my blood in a deplorable way.

"Count."

"One!" she shouted, fury drenching that single word. Even though her cunt was dripping, she still had the mind to be furious with me.

Hell, I loved her even more for it. Her fire, her spitting-nails spirit—she was the strap of leather that kept me in line. I tempered the beast inside me, and for the next few minutes, the world faded; it was just her, me, and the strikes of my belt that captured us in a bubble no force on Earth could penetrate. I was so caught up in the way she responded, transfixed by the lines crisscrossing her bottom, I almost forgot Jax was in the room with us, standing just outside our bubble.

I let loose another *whack*, but she failed to count. I rounded the bed and found her staring, unseeing, eyes glazed. Nearly unreachable. I lapped at her tears, running a palm over her hair, and gently grounded her. She sucked in a deep breath, sudden alertness widening her watery eyes.

"You okay?" How ludicrous a question, but I needed to know I wasn't pushing her *too* far. Though the idea that I hadn't, that maybe I never could push her beyond what she could handle, reeled me in, threatening to send me to the darkest corners of my mind. She was my fucking dream come true.

"I'm confused," she said.

"You're on eleven."

"No, I mean…I need to come…but it hurts too much."

I hadn't been certain how ginger would affect her, but apparently, it was intolerable in its burn…intolerable in other ways too.

It was fucking perfect.

"Eleven," I reminded her.

She blinked then recited, "Eleven."

I returned to my spot behind her vulnerable ass, widened my feet, and prepared to deliver number twelve. As I did so with my cock strutting its stuff, standing proudly above my shoved down sweats, motion caught my attention from the corner of my eye.

Jax wasn't staring at Alex or even the belt I fisted. He fastened his gaze on my cock, hastily unbuttoned his pants and lowered the zipper, and his hand went to work. His eyes darted to mine for a second—less than a fucking second—before he dropped his gaze.

And I realized he felt awkward, maybe even ashamed for ogling me, for being turned on by watching. Strangely, I didn't feel the same way. I might have before we'd shared a cell for three years, but we'd had so little privacy in that cramped space, there wasn't anything he *hadn't* seen.

He'd been there all the times I'd curled into a ball, muffling my trauma into the pillow as my ass flamed from a slew of intruding cocks. He'd sat with me silently, not touching, just being there and listening as I tried to hold it in but couldn't.

He'd given me his understanding without saying a word.

Though, at the time, I hadn't understood how he could grasp even a sliver of the tormented headspace I'd fallen into. But now, having seen firsthand how he'd been raised…he'd known more about it than he'd let on.

I struck Alex again, and her muttered *thirteen* broke the trance for me. Though not for Jax. His head fell back against the wall, his lids at half-mast, mouth parted as he pumped his cock.

I eyed Alex's reddened skin, yearning to watch her squirm for the last seven lashes, but she wouldn't do that as long as the ginger tamed her movement. I worked it from her rectum, making her hiss in a breath, and for the final leg of her punishment, I put extra strength into those strikes.

She shrieked. She bucked. She cried. She pleaded for me to stop. She begged for me to keep going. I sent her spiraling through her mind, unable to stop tumbling head over end. Dropping the belt at my feet with a loud *thump*, I stood directly behind her, rubbing my cock between the valley of her ass cheeks.

"Baby," I ground out between clenched teeth. *Oh shit...*

I'd lost my grasp on control. Two rough pumps of my hand spelled the end of me, and I spilled all over her backside. Breathing way too fucking fast, I pummeled her cunt with one hand and rubbed my cum into her silky smooth skin with the other. This took the idea of finger painting to new heights. She arched her spine, screeching a plea for mercy that collided with Jax's quiet grunts of release.

And my dick wasn't done yet, apparently. A sexually

charged dungeon of sin existed between these walls, and I was the warden. Before I made the mistake of thrusting into her, I released her arms and legs with jittery fingers, drawing noisy breaths that surely sucked all the fucking oxygen from the room.

Jax sent me a stricken expression before he left without saying a single word. Shit. After this, we would have stuff to deal with, but right now I had my hands full. Literally. I couldn't keep them off her gorgeous ass.

She'd spread her arms out like wings, spent from the torment I'd unleashed onto her body, but also panting with the need to come. She pushed her ass even further into my palms, moaning, practically begging me to fuck her.

"Please," she gasped. "I need to come. Don't leave me like this."

I wanted to give her what she wanted; my cock inside her and the air splintering with her cries of pleasure. But this was meant to be a punishment, and I'd already fucked up once when it came to her. I strode to the dresser, grabbed the white bag Jax had given me, and pulled out the instructions.

"Says here I can't fuck you bareback for a few days." I let out a low curse. "I'm not about to knock you up." I helped her to her feet, and something about the way her skirt cascaded to shield her body irritated the fuck out of me. I wanted to rip that flowing material to shreds.

Instead, I shoved the bag and the paper into her shaking hands then twirled her around toward the bathroom. "I want you on those pills pronto. And be sure to take the morning after pill too. Get cleaned up," I ordered, smacking her ass.

Go, I mentally screamed, before I did something stupid...again.

17. AFTERSHOCKS

ALEX

The faint sound of the bathroom door sliding shut clued me into his presence. I closed my eyes and let the shower spray run down my face, washing away my tears, hoping it would drive away the filth corrupting every inch of my body and soul.

I hated him.

No...I *wanted* to hate him. But he was Rafe Mason, the one man capable of possessing me. He could get away with murder, and I'd forgive it. I circled myself in the shelter of my arms, attempting to create a fortress even he couldn't bypass. What a joke. I failed to crack from being used and beaten—instead, I crumbled when denied the privilege of getting off on it.

God that was messed up on so many levels.

"Are you okay?" Apology laced his words. Rafe the gentle protector was back, not to say I didn't love Rafe the twisted asshat too.

Because I did.

I loved all of him, and maybe that's why I was so upset. He'd let Jax lay his hands on me. He'd made me cry, scream, and beg for the burn of ginger to just *stop*. Instead of showing me mercy, he'd taken his pound of flesh before taunting me with the warm, thick evidence of his release all over my ass. Maybe that's what I was really pissed about—the throb between my legs that still imprisoned me.

"I took the stupid pills if that's what you're worried about."

He entered the tiny space and wrapped his arms around me, his naked chest flush with my back. "I'm worried about *you*." He captured my wrists in his hands, and I slowly unraveled in his embrace as the tension in my muscles melted away. He clung to me as if he'd never let go.

"Don't be," I said. "You got your message across. I won't go against you again."

He grabbed my chin and turned my face, bringing my gaze to his. "Are you upset over the ginger, Jax's involvement, or that I didn't let you come?"

I gritted my teeth, refusing to respond.

"Answer me, or I won't answer your questions."

I let out a shallow breath. I'd nearly forgotten. "I'm upset with myself."

"Why?"

"Because you fucking hurt me, and I wanted to come!"

He slid his fingers down my throat and gripped my neck, holding me inside his gaze, victim to the cage of his body. Water drenched his hair, and God, he was the epitome of sexy. It was *not* fair.

"Ask your questions," he said in that gruff tone that made my insides quiver.

I gave myself a firm mental shake because I knew what he was doing. He wanted to have this conversation while he had all the power. While he was a squeeze away from choking me. While I was the vulnerable one because opening up to me would strip him bare.

I swallowed under the weight of his control, finding my voice. "Why did you leave six months ago?"

His gaze faltered. "I should've known you'd start with that."

Well, duh. I bit my tongue to keep from saying it out loud.

"I killed Perrone," he said, his strangled admission nearly drowned out by the spray of the shower. He drew in a quick breath. "I snapped, Alex. I stabbed him with his own fucking pen, but it wasn't enough. I wanted to squeeze his damn head off." He fell silent for a while.

"You're still not telling me why you left," I said after the seconds stretched into a full minute.

"I got my memory back."

"Rafe," I whispered, freeing my hand from his. I slid my palm along the side of his face. "You could have told me." Drops of water hung from his thick lashes, bringing out the vulnerability in his eyes. It was hard to believe this was the same guy who'd blasted my ass not more than a half hour ago.

"I remembered every disgusting thing I'd done to you." Shuttering his eyes, he leaned into my palm and let out a broken sigh. "And even with that bastard's blood on my hands, his fucking house in flames, I just wanted to lose myself in you, but I couldn't."

"Why not?"

"I didn't trust myself. Those eight years flooded in, and it was just…"

"Too much?"

"Yeah. I wasn't thinking."

He'd gone into run mode. I could relate because that's what I'd done yesterday. The only difference was I'd gotten punished for it. But something told me he'd been punishing himself since the day he'd taken off. He'd stayed away because the guy hiding behind his memory loss had terrified him.

"Next question," he said, clearly wanting to shut

down this particular thread.

I wasn't about to let him off that easily. "Tell me what happened in prison."

His body went rigid, and he glared at me. "No."

"You promised me the truth."

He slid his hand down my belly and brushed his fingers over my throbbing clit. "How about I take care of this instead?"

"How about you stop using sex to get your way? After everything we've been through, I deserve your honesty, don't you think?"

Abruptly, he let me go. "Why are you doing this?" He slid to the cool tile, holding his head in his hands. Without hesitation, I sank to my knees in front of him, though I sensed his need for space, so I didn't touch him, despite the cramped stall making *not* touching him difficult.

"Because I love you. I want you to unload on me." Because I was the reason he'd gone through hell in that place.

He dragged his hands through his hair and shot me a hard look. "Should I demand you tell me what Zach did to you? Make you recount all the fucking details? Make you relive it?"

"You're deflecting."

"So what if I am? Some things should stay in the past. This is one of those things, Alex."

"Not if it's putting walls between us." I trailed my fingers across my throat. "Not if it's giving you nightmares."

"You're scared of me." His gaze followed the path of my fingers, a reminder of how he'd choked me in his sleep. "I might push you, sweetheart, but I never want you to be afraid of me."

"I'm not." I let my hand drop. Even his subconscious would pull through to protect me because that's who he was. He'd attacked me in his sleep, but he'd *stopped*. "I startled you during that nightmare."

"What do you mean?"

"I grabbed your shoulder. That's when you came at me."

"I can't..." He shook his head. "Babe, I managed to sleep next to you at your house last night without a problem, but I can't risk that happening again."

"It won't. You don't have it in you to really hurt me, Rafe. Besides," I said, placing my hand on his arm. "I know better now. I'll turn on a light or something next time."

"There can't be a next time." He pushed to his feet in a single, fluid move and pulled me up. "Let's continue this conversation later. You can ask your last question then."

I frowned. "I still have two left. You never answered the second one, so it doesn't count."

"In my book, it does. I answered you, honestly, and I

honestly think we don't need to go there, ever."

"Forget the stupid questions." Trying not to glower at him, I retreated and bumped into the side of the stall. "Why can't you just talk to me? Is it that hard to have a conversation like a normal couple?"

"We're not normal."

"No, but maybe we should sprinkle a little normal on this…whatever *this* is."

He shut the water off with an angry downward strike of his hand. "Don't try to change me into something I'm not." His eyes raked over my erect nipples and the water dripping off of them. "We are who we are."

"I want more. I need more from you!"

Biting back a frustrated growl, he wrenched me by the arm and pulled me from the bathroom, into the bedroom, and bent me over the bed again. A piece of me died right there. My ass was already raw from the last punishment. How much more did he need to dole out? How much more did he think I could take?

Blinking silent tears down my cheeks, I closed my eyes to the sound of a drawer sliding open and slamming shut. His footfalls thundered across the room, and at the first touch of his hand on my bottom, I tensed, my misery and fear and anger tearing from my lips, unbidden.

But…

What the hell?

"Relax," he said, voice soft, almost tender, and it tore

my heart out just to set it in place again. "Even animals can be tamed." He rubbed something into my skin that soothed my burning welts.

My legs trembled violently, and I cried in earnest, this time out of pure relief. More tears escaped, but not because I was sad, hurt or even scared. His touch reassured me that the man I'd fallen even more in love with while trapped in that tunnel still existed. The man who'd take care of me. Protect me. Love me.

"Do you hate me for what I did earlier?" Uncertainty tinged his voice, and it was so fucking surreal, this constant battle he seemed to be in with himself.

I chewed on my lip for a few moments, deliberating on how truthful I should be. Giving him my honesty would mean he'd only push harder in the future. Did I want that?

Maybe I did.

"I don't think there's anything you can do that will make me hate you."

He pulled me up by the shoulders, apparently satisfied that my ass was taken care of. "I know you want more from me, babe. I wanna give you more. I wanna give you fucking everything." He stalked to the dresser, his steps taking on the weight of importance, urgency. He pulled out two sets of clothing—one for him and one for me.

"There's something I need to do before this fight, and I want you there with me for it."

18. FAMILY MATTERS

RAFE

"Why are we here?" she asked, keeping her voice low as we entered the gymnasium. I appreciated her desire to remain low key. I'd told her on the way in that I didn't want to be spotted, especially as the once famous Rafe "The Choker" Mason. But instinctively, I knew her need to be invisible stemmed from more than my wish for her to do so.

She *wanted* to be invisible because it provided safety. She'd tried to remain as unobtrusive as possible for most of her life. That innate need of hers came in handy now, but eventually, once the dust settled and we found some sort of normalcy in the chaos of our lives, I'd make her shine. I'd demand she stand out like the amazing fucking diamond she was.

But today wasn't that day. As I threaded our fingers and burrowed deeper into my hoodie, I kept my head low and led her through the throng of people arriving for the basketball game.

If I could escape a fucking underground sex trafficking tunnel with little more than a hoodie, then I shouldn't have a problem watching my son's game without raising too much suspicion. I'd spied him leaving school, had even followed him home to his grandparent's humongous house on the hill, but this was the closest I'd had the nerve to venture.

Maybe having Alex at my side gave me the nudge I needed...because I had to see him one last time before Alex and I disappeared.

I *had* to know he was doing okay.

"Rafe?" she questioned again.

"C'mon." I stepped up the bleachers, pulling her behind me. She hastened to match my long strides as I climbed to the top right corner. I sat down and pulled her onto my lap.

She hissed a breath between clenched teeth, and my damn cock responded to the pain in her voice. Rather than shift so her tender ass would settle more comfortably, I kept her planted there. Resting my chin on her shoulder, I let her shield my identity. Hopefully, people would only see two lovebirds cuddling in the back by themselves and not question why no one seemed to know the unfamiliar faces among them.

This hole of a town on the Oregon coast, where Will's grandparent's lived, wasn't big, but the school wasn't dinky either, since city hall had combined grades K through eight.

Sneakers pitter-pattered on the court below, and balls bounced, echoing off the walls. Some of the kids had arrived to warm up, but Will wasn't among them yet. I drew in a deep breath and wrapped my arms around Alex's middle, holding on to her for strength. For courage.

"You're shaking," she whispered.

"I'm scared as fuck." That wasn't easy for me to admit.

She went still in my arms. "What are we doing here?"

Will entered, and I swallowed my nervousness. Fuck, he'd grown so much since the last time I'd seen him hopping into his grandmother's van four weeks ago. At least, he seemed taller. I recalled the first time I'd laid eyes on him in Dante's Pass, right after I'd gotten out of prison. Those inquisitive green eyes had stared at me from the back of Nikki's Toyota, painting the picture of a boy fascinated by the stranger who'd chased his mother down the sidewalk.

Like always, I wondered if he missed her, which was a stupid thing to wonder because I'd missed my mom like crazy after she left.

But Nikki was dead.

How the fuck was he coping? Shit, I couldn't even be there for him because I was partly responsible for what had happened to Nikki.

An anxious flutter went through me. How would Alex react once she learned I had a son? I already knew she'd blame herself for Nikki's death, and I had no fucking idea how to deal with that, or how badly she'd self-destruct. And what the fuck was I supposed to say to her? She was partially to blame. We all were.

Letting out an aggravated sigh, Alex squirmed in my arms. "Talk to me." The pain in her voice cut me deep, and I wanted to kick myself. She didn't deserve to be shut out like this. Sliding my palms along the backs of her small hands, I tracked the sprinting form of Will with my gaze.

"You see that boy down there dribbling the ball? Number 44?"

She scanned the kids until she found him. "Yeah?"

I entwined our fingers, knowing there wasn't an easy way to say this. "He's my son, Alex."

She went still, and if not for the screeching sound of sneakers on a polished floor, or the joyous whoops from the kids below, I was certain the silence would've been deafening.

"What…?" She shook her head, mouth agape.

"Huh?"

Brushing my lips over her ear, I whispered the truth. How Nikki discovered she was pregnant after I'd gone to prison. How she hadn't told me until I'd gotten out. How I'd forgotten that conversation, along with everything else, until after Perrone killed her in front of us.

"I just knew. I couldn't remember shit about the rest of those eight years, but I knew she had a kid." I let out a breath that ruffled her hair. "I knew he was mine."

"How?" Alex pulled her lips between her teeth. "I mean, how do you know for sure?"

"Look at him, babe."

She did, and her shoulders slumped the longer she studied him. She turned her head toward the exit, and I imagined the wheels turning in her head, figured she wanted through those doors rather than face reality with me.

"Why did you bring me here?"

Warm-up time on the court ended, and the kids readied for the start of the game. I spoke to Alex in low tones, my gaze glued to my son's every move. Between the scuffle of the game and the parents' excited shouts, no one paid us any attention.

"You want me to let you in, well…I wanted you to know," I told her. "I needed you to know."

"Why?"

"I'm winning this fight, Alex, and after it's done and

over with, I'm taking you outta here. But I couldn't leave without seeing him again. For his own good, he's a secret I intend to leave buried in my past, but I couldn't keep him from you."

Her body went rigid in my arms. "I'm the reason—" her voice cracked, and she sucked in a breath. "I'm the reason that boy down there doesn't have a mom." She dashed away a stray tear. "Or a dad."

I didn't want to miss the rest of the game or take my eyes off the boy who looked so much like me, but I could tell that Alex needed some space to process.

My son looked happy, adjusted, and that was all that mattered. I'd come to this area to be near him as much to outrun my demons, but it was time to move on. It nagged me like an impending storm that would pick me up and drop me three counties over in a whirlwind.

A person could only hide for so long.

As Will jumped and sent the ball sailing through the hoop, I urged Alex to her feet. We stepped down the bleachers with careful footfalls, trying not to draw attention to ourselves. Pushing the doors open, my son's shout of triumph rang through my ears as we headed toward the parking lot.

It might be the last time I heard his voice again, and I'd never forget it, or the glint in his eyes after he scored for his team. Those branded memories would have to last me a lifetime because he was better off never knowing me.

We strode into the chilly air, and Alex's wind-blown hair wiped the remnants of sorrow from her cheeks. She was silent the whole ride back to the boat. And fuck, she was pissing me off because I knew what she was doing.

Holding it in.

Her tears, her anger, her sadness.

"Let it out, baby," I said, rolling to a stop in the field. I shifted the truck into park.

"I could say the same to you," she said. "Why did you wait so long to tell me?"

"I wasn't sure how you'd take it. After what happened to Nik—"

She pushed the door open and hopped out. I flung the driver's side outward, and my feet hit the ground running. "Alex!"

She whirled, both hands grasping her hair. "You'd be with your son right now if it weren't for me. He'd have a mother!" She blinked rapidly, unraveling before my eyes and leaving me helpless to help her. "Oh my God!" she cried, and then the tears did spill over, rushing down her cheeks as if they wouldn't stop. "I did this!"

I wanted to reach out for her, tell her how wrong she was, but I couldn't. The what-ifs were endless, plaguing the back of my mind, and I knew they plagued the forefront of hers. Even so, I wasn't about to let her do this to herself.

"It's not your fucking fault! I don't know how many times I need to tell you that. I don't know when you'll actually hear me!"

"It *is* my fault!" she screamed, sliding her fingers under the sleeves of her jacket. I ground my teeth because I just fucking *knew* she was digging her nails in. "My lie destroyed more than just your life…" She hid her face in her hands.

I crossed the distance and shoved her toward the dock. She was too busy having a meltdown to pay attention to the water.

"Nikki, your son, the island, the vineyard…" she stuttered as our feet nearly skidded over the wet planks. "You've lost everything and everyone because of me."

"I still have you, don't I?" I hefted her over my shoulder and stepped onto the boat, almost careening into the rail, then stomped down the stairs into the cabin. I set her on her feet.

"No wonder you left me," she said, doubling over. "How can you stand to be near me?"

In two seconds flat, I had her wrists locked in my fists. "Look at me."

She shook her head. "I can't."

"I said look at me!" I gave her a firm shake until her burning eyes met mine. "You need to let it go. What's done is done. Punishing yourself isn't gonna change shit."

Her gaze landed on her bloodied fingernails. "But I

deserve everything that's happened to me. You don't deserve any of it. *I* did this, Rafe."

My heart pounded in my ears, at a level that rivaled a roar. "Is that why you get off on pain? Why you let Zach hurt you for so long? Why you let me?" I practically ripped the jacket from her body before pushing the sleeves of her shirt to her elbows. Jerking her by the arms, my gaze raked over her torn up skin. "This is the reason you keep fucking hurting yourself, isn't it? You think you deserve it."

"No, it's—"

"Yes it is!" I shook her again, my anger bubbling over, unstoppable. "I'll give you pain, babe. Any fucking time. Just say the fucking word."

But there would be no asking or pleading this time. I plopped onto the sofa, unbuttoned her jeans and yanked down the zipper, then bent her over my knee. I shoved the denim below her ass and brought my hand down with a loud whack. She cried out, but unlike with the ginger, her voice trilled with relief.

She needed this.

"You held onto that victim card like a trophy, not because you were helpless but because you thought you *deserved* it." I let another vicious smack fly on her ass.

She squirmed, moaning, and her skin flushed a gorgeous pink. I was spanking raw skin, still fresh with welts, but it didn't seem to bother her—not in the way it should. She was hot *and* bothered in a much different way. If I'd learned anything, it was that Alex was only punishable when denied what she wanted.

Me.

It had always been me.

My hand quaked with the need to lay into her harder, but I didn't want to go too far—not after the recent punishment Jax and I had put her through. But God help me. I'd spank her every fucking day until she stopped beating herself up. Until she stopped ripping into her skin. Until she finally forgave herself.

19. RICOCHET

ALEX

"Lex."

Something wasn't right—not just that I'd heard Zach call my name, but too much pressure built in my head. I was naked, my arms and legs bound by rope though it wasn't rough against my skin like I'd expect. The bindings hugged me, smooth as silk, pressing my ankles to the backs of my thighs, connecting to my wrists at my back.

Where the heck was I?

I parted my lips, but a feeble groan came out. The floor swayed underneath me.

No. I was the one moving, swinging upside down with my dark curls brushing the rough cement. A chair scraped behind me, and clothing rustled, drowned out by the soft thump of footsteps. I sensed the heat of his body before his clothes brushed my skin. Two sickeningly familiar palms kneaded my ass, fingers reaching close to the center of my traitorous cunt.

"Don't you fucking touch her!"

Rafe. I lifted my head and found him bound in chains.

Oh my God.

Nikki lay on the ground beside his feet in a puddle of blood.

We were back in the tunnel, only this time Zach was our tormenter.

I sobbed at the sight of Rafe. He sported a busted lip, and his left eye was swollen shut, lost to the ugly plum, mustard, and blue skin that puffed around his lid. And Nikki…she was dead. There was no saving her. We were all here because of me.

"She'll beg me to touch her," Zach said, running a finger up my slit. I was beet red with shame, afraid to look at Rafe because I'd only find repulsion.

"This changes nothing, babe. Do you hear me?" Rafe shouted. "You're mine. You'll always be mine."

Zach stomped across the room and shoved a cloth between Rafe's teeth. When he turned around, he did so with a devious smile. He sauntered to me, unbuttoning his jeans and yanking his zipper down to reveal his erection springing toward me at eye-level.

"I know you love us both," Zach said, gripping my head so I couldn't turn away, "but you have a decision to make."

"What decision?" I cried, my eyes stinging.

"You need to decide which one of us gets to live."

I jerked awake with a silent scream, mouth wide open

in horror. Huffing in fast and shallow breaths, I gazed at Rafe's side of the bed and found it empty. The clock glowed an eerie 12:02 a.m.

We'd gone to bed over an hour ago, but where was he?

Sliding from the sweat-drenched sheets, I tiptoed into the sitting area and found him festering in the dark.

"Rafe?" My voice came out hollow, small, and I had to say his name again before he realized I stood in the shadows, burrowing into them, finding comfort in the obscurity of blackness.

How strange that darkness comforted at a time like this, right after I'd awakened thrashing in the sheets, sweat drenching my skin, unable to scream because terror had lodged in my throat. I raised my hand, then halted half way to my arm, nails aching to dig in.

Rafe and I exchanged a meaningful glance, and I dropped my hand. But the need to get lost in the sting of pain was overbearing, strangling...strong enough to make a person go mad. I ached to feel his hand on my ass, but I didn't think I deserved it—not after the twisted dreams I'd been having for the past few nights.

Since the day Rafe revealed his son to me, life had gone on in an odd, surreal way. I'd spent my days chained to the bedroom floor while he left to train for the upcoming match with Zach. Nothing I said or did would change his mind about fighting my brother.

He said he was doing it for me...for us. But I didn't believe him. He harbored an immeasurable amount of rage. Since Rafe had decided not to take it out on me, Zach was the only one left, the true culprit—in Rafe's eyes—responsible for everything. For his imprisonment, the destruction of his family's legacy, and even the murder of his son's mother.

But we weren't on the same page. We weren't even in the same book. I'd had a choice; lie or tell the truth, and I'd made the wrong call. The worst decision of my life had ricocheted for years, not only destroying Rafe but the lives of so many others. Maybe he could forgive me for it, make excuses for my reprehensible behavior, but I couldn't forgive myself no matter how often he spanked me or demanded I let the guilt go. Nothing had the power to abolish this sense of culpability I carried around, and it was manifesting in my dreams.

The first night I dreamed of Zach's tongue between my thighs, I thought I'd vomit all over Rafe as he slept at my side. How I managed to silence my disgusted sobs without waking him, I didn't know. I'd toyed with the idea of telling him, especially when he gave me a certain look —like he knew something was wrong and I was keeping it from him.

"Why are you out here?" I asked.

"Couldn't sleep. Too keyed up, I guess."

I gulped. The fight was tomorrow. A few hours ago,

he'd received a text alerting him to keep an eye out for another text disclosing the time and location. No wonder he couldn't sleep. No wonder I was having bad dreams.

We were living in a real life nightmare.

He rose slowly, and his bare feet padded across the space. He set two gentle hands on my shoulders. So gentle, yet those fingers could wield crushing strength around my throat, were immovable when they held my chin in place during a lecture.

"What's wrong?" he asked, studying my face. If I told him nothing was wrong, he'd know. This was *it*—the moment I'd known was coming. He was about to force my hand.

But I *wanted* to be open with him. I wanted to be able to tell him anything and everything, the way I expected him to. Fair was fair.

"I…" Clearing my throat, I tried again, but nothing came out.

He frowned. "What do you need from me, babe? Tell me."

"You know what I need. Don't make me say it."

"Not only are you gonna say it, but you're gonna beg for it." He lowered his face, hungry lips lingering close.

Too close.

I couldn't decide if I wanted to kiss him, or bend over and offer him my ass.

"Hurt me," I whispered. "Please, Rafe. Hurt me in a

way that makes me feel good."

"Get on your knees," he said, his palms applying pressure to my shoulders. Allowing my knees to buckle, I lowered to my haunches. The floor welcomed me with unbearable hardness. I squirmed, spread my thighs, and clasped my hands at my back, the way I knew he liked.

Not many would understand how cherished I felt at that moment when he commanded my eyes and brushed his fingers through my curls.

"I was hoping you'd tell me on your own, but you've been silently stewing for days. Enough is enough. What's bothering you?"

I opened my mouth, but words failed me. How could I tell him about the dreams without sounding like a total whore?

"I've been having nightmares."

"Okay," he said with patience, trailing his fingers through my hair still, nearly hypnotizing me with his touch. "Unload them on me."

I dropped my gaze to his feet. "I don't...I can't remember details."

"You're lying to me." His fingers curled at my scalp and pulled in warning. "You know how that will end."

I wanted to deny it, but I couldn't bring myself to perpetuate the lie. "Don't make me tell you this." I swallowed past the lump of shame clogging my throat. "I'm naked, on my knees, willing to do anything. What more do you want from me?"

"The truth. Isn't that how this works? You're not weaseling your way out of this one. If you need the bite of pain, I'll give it to you. But I want to know why first. You're not punishing yourself anymore. That's my burden now."

"I'm not punishing my—"

"Do I need to make your ass burn for lying?"

"No," I said quickly, cringing at the thought of my bottom flaming from ginger. That was probably the one thing I despised most. The pain of his belt or hand gave me the sting I craved…needed, but the intensity of that evil stuff was beyond my limits.

"Then start talking. This is the third night you've had a nightmare. What's haunting you?"

I hadn't realized he'd known. And here I thought I'd been clever by keeping the dreams to myself. I shifted, gritting my teeth against the floor under my knees. "Can I get up first?"

He pulled the waistband of his pajama pants below his hard-on. "Give me your mouth, and I'll think about it." He yanked on my curls and drew me closer to his straining shaft. "When you're ready to confess what's really bothering you, I'll let you get up. Until then, I'm gonna make you choke on my cock. I've got a lot of stamina built up, so you might be down there for a while."

I peeked at his imposing form. God, he was beautiful.

That expanse of muscle and the sexy lines of ink that was as much a part of him as his domineering nature.

"Open your mouth," he said, his voice raspy, breathless. Caging me between his body and the wall, he shot a palm out and propped himself up as he nudged my lips with his erection.

I felt undeniably exposed with my legs spread wide and my hands at my back. Heat flared at my center, but there would be no relief until I spilled. Just empty space and chilly air to tease me. I fastened my lips around him, drawing in a deep breath, and gave up on the idea of begging him for what I wanted, needed.

His belt on my ass.

Him telling me I wasn't a worthless, unlovable whore.

Him inside me. Now.

God, I needed all those things more than my next breath, so I sucked his cock with vigor, laving my tongue on the underside of his shaft, around the head, flicking lightly over the slit, before taking him deep. Over and over again—lick, swirl, flick, and suck him hard. All the while, I kept my gaze latched on his face.

"Your mouth is fucking heaven." He groaned, neck straining as he tilted his head back. He fisted my hair and pulled me closer, plunging past my tonsils. I gagged, struggling not to struggle, and gagged again. I whined around his shaft, my eyes burning from the position he'd forced me into.

"*Fuck*. Feels so good when you gag."

Shit, I was in trouble. I closed my eyes and tried not to panic, reminding myself that this was Rafe, and he wouldn't hurt me.

He just had tastes.

Don't panic.

I sucked in air through my nose and tried to get my gag reflex under control. Another long groan splintered the air, and he started thrusting.

Fast.

Hard.

Like a driven man.

Then he tempered the rhythm, pushing between my lips slow and gentle like he had all the time in the world to fuck my mouth.

Stamina, he'd said. He wasn't kidding.

But this was about more than getting head. I'd waited too long to come to him, had suffered in silence and hid the reason. That's why he was so worked up, so pissed off. I'd demanded he open up to me in the shower, then I'd turned around and done the opposite.

He sped up the tempo again, plundering my mouth until my eyes stung from the pain. I wrung my fingers behind me to keep from shoving him away because that would only make this worse for me. My job was to kneel and take it. So I took his cock and ignored the slurping noises escaping my lips. He slipped in and out, and each time he hit the back of my throat, I dry-heaved, a thrust away from vomiting. *Let it be over soon.*

Without warning, he pulled out.

"You ready to tell me the truth now?"

After the rough blowjob, my head was in a fog. I searched through my mind for what it was he wanted me to tell him. Zach. The dreams. How the hell could I confess now, especially when he had me on my knees with his cock in my face?

"It's the fight. I've been having nightmares about it." At least it was partially true.

He scrutinized my face, seeming to consider my words. "You're a shitty liar."

"Rafe, please—" He silenced me with his cock again, his hooded green eyes peering at me, irises dark and vacant, save for the rampant need in them.

"Do you know what happens when you lie to me?" With a raspy grunt, he held my head in place as he positioned his tip between my lips. "You get your mouth washed out." His fingers tightened in my hair. "I'm gonna come," he said, groaning. "Hold it in your mouth. Do *not* spit or swallow."

My eyes widened as he pumped his release onto my tongue. The way he threw his head back, eyes closed in ecstasy, ignited me. But this wasn't about my pleasure—this was a way for him to punish me for lying to him.

He slipped out inch by inch. I pressed my lips

together and hollowed out my cheeks, so I didn't spill any of his hot, thick cum.

"Don't move." He stalked into the bedroom, and I heard him rifling through the drawers. He returned with a fistful of clothespins, and my stomach dropped. A chill of fear and anticipation swept over me. I felt ridiculous with my cheeks rounded out, full of his jizz.

"You'd better keep that mouth full because I have ginger waiting to be used in the fridge if you don't." He pulled me to my feet, ran a finger along my slit, and a dark smile graced his face. "While you're thinking about how you got yourself into this predicament, I'm gonna play with your cunt—your very beautiful, very wet cunt—but you aren't coming until I give you permission. Got it?"

I nodded, and he brushed his thumb over my mouth. A small amount of his cum dribbled down my chin.

"You know better than to waste any of that." Grabbing a clothespin between his thumb and forefinger, he clamped it over my nose.

I tried so fucking hard not to panic, squirming instead of opening my mouth as my lungs burned for air. But holy hell, if it didn't take every last ounce of self-control I had to hold the position. His salty cum collected at my lips, threatening to trickle out.

"Are you in control here?" he asked, his gaze pinning me more than the strongest pair of cuffs would.

I jerked my head back and forth.

"Am I in control here, sweetheart?"

"Mmm-hmmm," I moaned, bobbing my head.

"Next time you think it's a good idea to lie to me, you'd better be ready for the consequences."

My heart thundered in my ears, and I was mere seconds away from spewing his cum all over the both of us. I *needed* to breathe!

As if my huge eyes imparted my desperate need for oxygen, he removed the pin. I sucked air through my nose, pulling it deep into my lungs, and thought my heart would pound right out of my chest.

But Rafe wasn't done playing with me. He trailed his fingertips down the sides of my breasts, over my ribcage, and dipped a finger into my drenched center. Twisting my nipple between his teeth, he pulled, all the while keeping his eyes on mine. Grabbing another clothespin, he released my nipple and clamped it. The grip of that clothespin was torture, yet I liquefied even more around his finger moving in and out of me in unhurried slides.

His lips followed the valley between my breasts as he journeyed to the other side. I tensed, preparing for the pain of his teeth, followed by another clothespin. He seemed to take forever drawing my nipple outward until I could hardly stand the pain. By the time he fastened the second makeshift clamp, my other nipple had gone blessedly numb.

"I love your tits. I love your ass. I love everything about you. I love how you're holding my cum in your mouth, just because I said so. I fucking love how you're taking the pain." He palmed his hard shaft. "Look what you do to me. My cock is incapable of quitting you."

I blinked against the burn in my eyes, hating my slow surrender to the pull of his words.

"Rule number four," he reminded me with a growl.

Just like that, the floodgates opened, and my tears hung on my lashes. Then they spilled over so his ravenous tongue could feast on them.

20. NOBODY PRAYING FOR ME

RAFE

The salt of her tears sent me into a frenzy, and my insufferable cock twitched at the taste. I was free to fuck her now without the worry of fathering another kid. I wondered if she realized that. I hoped she did, because if she forced me to punish her with ginger again…

Damn it to hell. I didn't want to do it. I wanted her to be real with me so we could tumble into bed and forget the fucking world existed for a while.

"Spit, babe. I wanna see my cum all over those beautiful tits." I wanted to make sure she hadn't discreetly swallowed; the show was a bonus.

Parting her lips, she let my cum dribble over her chin and onto her heaving tits. Her hair cascaded around her

GEMMA JAMES

shoulders, curls a tempting tangled mess that teased her pink cheeks.

"Fuck, you're gorgeous." I removed the clothespins from her nipples, loving the way she hissed air between her teeth from the sudden rush of blood. "Let's try this again. What's bothering you?"

She twisted her head to the side. Sensing how difficult this was for her, I allowed her that bit of space while I grabbed a towel from the galley.

"Do I need to get the ginger out?" I asked as I passed her the hand towel.

The frantic shake of her head was immediate. Even so, she took her time wiping my cum off her tits, and I knew she was stalling

"Babe, my cum isn't the only thing you need to get off your chest."

"I've been having dreams about Zach."

I wanted to punish her ass into next Sunday upon hearing those words. "What kind of dreams?"

"The kind that…" She gulped. "They're sick. I don't understand them." She shook her head. "Please, Rafe. I'm begging you. Let this go."

"No fucking way in hell. You're gonna tell me every last detail."

"They're sexual." She nibbled on her lip. "He's doing things to me."

"What kind of *things*?" I asked between gritted teeth.

172

She closed her eyes but was unable to hide her pain. I gathered her in my arms and sent myself a swift kick in the ass for being such an idiot. She was trying so hard to obey me, and I wasn't making this easy.

"Just tell me," I said, softening my tone.

"We're back in the tunnel. I'm upside down, tied up. You're in chains. Nikki's there—" Her voice fractured.

I slid a hand into her hair, grasping her by the nape. "Go on."

"Zach's taunting you, touching me…"

Her arms snaked around me, holding on tight, and I let out a sigh. The dreams had disturbed her deeply, and not because she still wanted Zach, but because he was a fucking lunatic that scared her.

Why I couldn't get that to stick, I might never know.

Her quick intake of breath told me there was more. Afraid of rattling her further, I remained silent and waited.

"Call off the fight. Rafe, please. I'll do anything. I'll let you torture me with ginger, let you fuck me any way you want—"

"You'll already let me do that."

"That's beside the point!" She shot me a seething glare. "Don't do this, I'm begging you. Call off the fight."

"I can't. There's too much at play here. Too much at stake. You have to understand—"

"I understand one of you is going to die!" She shoved

against my chest, putting all her strength into untangling herself from my embrace. "And I don't want it to be you."

"You want Zach dead then?" I asked, raising a speculative brow. "Is that what you're saying?"

She shuffled back, and I wanted to shake an answer from her because my sanity, everything I was, hinged on what fell from those luscious lips.

Lips still damp from my cum.

Fuck, she was the distraction from hell.

"That's not what I meant."

My heart plopped somewhere in my gut. "What *do* you mean, then?"

She retreated. I advanced. We'd been perfecting this dance for ages, it seemed.

"I don't wanna see anyone else hurt."

"Even Zach?"

She licked her lips then sucked her lower one between her teeth.

"Answer me," I snapped, my attention captured by her mouth and thoughts of what it did to me.

"Even him."

"After everything that piece of shit has done, why would you want me to spare him?"

"It's not about him, Rafe. God! It's about you! You're better than this. You're not a fucking murderer."

"I killed Perrone," I pointed out.

A hint of uncertainty washed over her pale face. "Self-defense, no doubt."

She had no fucking clue. I'd scorched her ass with ginger. Allowed another man to beat her. I'd fucked her in the ass against her wishes, yet she still didn't see what stood right in front of her.

"I'm a monster, Alex. I choked Jax's uncle in prison. I hunted Brock down and choked him to death too. Still think I'm better than this?"

She jerked her head back and forth, eyes wide. Disbelieving. She backed up another step and stumbled into the wall.

"I know who you are in here," she said, placing a trembling hand over her heart. "Your capacity to forgive tells me all I need to know about you. I don't know what road you've been down these past few months, but this is not you." She was clinging to denial of epic proportions.

"It is me, babe." I launched myself at her, caging her in, giving off an intimidating vibe even she couldn't deny. "I want to kill him." I grabbed her chin and lowered my face to hers, and our lips nearly met. "It kills me that you don't want it too. He deserves nothing less than death."

She swallowed hard. "We all deserve things, Rafe."

"What would you have me do then, huh? Let the fucker kill me and take off with you?"

Her eyes widened, then something I couldn't name passed over her features. "A decision," she muttered. "I choose you. Always. Do what you have to do, but don't you dare forget who you are." She slid her palm up my abs and stalled at my galloping heartbeat. "Don't forget who you are in *here*. You're the love of my life, Rafe. The guy I've been head over heels for since before I knew what love was."

"Fuck, baby." I buried my face in her shoulder, overcome with…just fucking overcome. "I don't want you to hate me."

"Impossible," she whispered. "I have no choice but to love you."

21. ODE TO 1:11

RAFE

We fucked before she fell asleep in my arms. Though *fucked* might be the wrong word. More like falling into each other, body and fucking soul. She had a piece of me I'd never get back, and I figured the same was true for her too. I carefully removed my arms from her body and rolled onto my back. Maybe I should have pushed her sooner about the dreams, but I knew firsthand how dredging up nightmares could sear straight through someone. Mine, thank fuck, had taken a vacation.

My cell vibrated on the nightstand next to the clock glowing a neon green 1:11 a.m. Not many people called me, and only one would at this hour. I grabbed my phone, eased from the bed, and crept through the door before answering.

"What's up?"

"You awake?"

"I am now."

"Sorry," Jax said, cursing under his breath. "I know you have the fight tomorrow to worry about. I just…"

Something about his tone put me on alert. "What's wrong?"

"I got a lead on Tawny. Gotta go back to Mexico."

"Don't even think about picking up an extra passenger this time." Though he'd have difficulty getting to Zach with Shelton hiding him somewhere.

"I ain't touching him, okay? I'm just saying… goodbye, I guess."

"Wait. You're leaving *now*?"

"She's my sister. I've gotta find her."

"I know that, Jax. I just didn't realize you were taking off in the middle of the fucking night."

A long pause blared between us. "You should do the same. Take Alex and just go. I don't have a good feeling about this, man. Shelton's a sketchy dude." He'd been saying that from day one. Jax had never liked the guy.

"You're sketchy," I pointed out.

"No denying that."

He agreed with me too easily. And maybe it was true. Jax was a sketchy bastard, but I saw myself in him. He wrestled with demons, same as me. We were kindred spirits.

"Don't lose my number," I said. "Let me know if you find her. I'll be heading out of here right after the fight."

"I'll call you when I know something." Another beat passed. "Be careful tomorrow night."

The call went dead, and I stared at the phone for a few seconds, astonished he'd hung up on me. Obviously, he had other things on his mind, but I guessed it was more than his sister. Like Alex, he didn't want to see me participate in this fight.

I tiptoed back to the bedroom and checked on her, relieved to find that she hadn't stirred.

Jax was right. I should pack a bag, grab her, and just go. Every atom in my body screamed at me to do so…yet here I stood. It was like that morning six months ago when Jax and I prepared to break into Perrone's estate. Despite the sick feeling in my gut, I'd promised Alex something I shouldn't have promised her.

I said I'd come back.

I prayed to fuck I wasn't destined to repeat history. I'd told her I was going to win this fight, and I had every intention of doing so. Whether Zach left the cage on his feet or in a body bag…that, I didn't know. But I was ready for this match, believed the odds were in my favor, and I'd never had better motivation.

Take Alex and just go.

Those words became a chant in my head. Fuck, he

was right. *Alex* was right. They were so fucking right it was insane. What was I trying to prove? It didn't matter. Nothing was as important as keeping her safe.

I didn't remember spanning the floor between the doorway and the closet, but suddenly I was pulling out a duffle, yanking drawers open, and tossing shit into the bag. We could be out of here in fifteen minutes, twenty tops. Just fucking disappear in the middle of the night, and no one would miss us for hours. Zach didn't know where the safe house was, and neither did Shelton. Jax was the only one who knew, and as far as sketchy people went, he was the only sketchy person I'd trust with my life. He hadn't told a soul about that house, and he wouldn't.

Alex and I could lay low for a few days while I emptied out my accounts, assuming I still had access to them. People might wonder why a missing person was suddenly pulling out money from—

"What are you doing?" Alex's sleepy voice cut into the manic thoughts racing on the tracks of my mind.

"Get dressed. We're getting the fuck outta here."

She sprang upright. "You're not fighting?" Her voice sounded hopeful, which only made me feel shittier.

"No, I shouldn't have let things get this far. You're right. We need to get moving." If Zach were stupid enough to come after us, I'd kill him without hesitation or remorse.

She jumped out of bed and hastily dressed in a pair of jeans and a sweatshirt. Her hair was a mess, but she didn't seem to care, and I sure as hell didn't care because she looked damn sexy with those locks twisted in a wild array around her face.

She had a thoroughly fucked look about her I'd never get enough of. Before I changed my mind about fleeing, I zipped up the duffle, grabbed my gun—the one that had faired better than Alex's purse—and we made our way through the dark toward the stairs.

Fierce cold wind blasted us on deck. I flung the bag over my shoulder, tucked the gun into the waistband of my jeans, and adjusted her hood to protect her face from the bitter weather. "You okay?"

"Just get me on land."

Winding an arm around her, I pulled her to my side, and we stepped off the boat together, shuffled down the slick dock, and ventured into soggy grass. We trudged through the mud toward my truck, parked mere feet away.

A pair of headlights illuminated us in the night. Pushing Alex behind me, I halted as doors opened and slammed shut. Two men ambled toward us, carefree. Like we were good friends, except the guns they grasped at their sides told a different story. At least they weren't fucking pointing them at us yet, and I wanted to keep it that way.

"Fuck, you scared the shit outta me," I said,

recognizing Nate.

"What's going on?" He gestured toward the bag hanging over my shoulder.

"Just putting some stuff in the truck for tomorrow." I glanced at Alex and tried to convey how dire this situation might become if she didn't play along. "Babe, you wanna put this in the truck? Should be unlocked."

With a nervous swallow, she took the duffle and tromped through the mud. I shuffled sideways, keeping me between Alex and our intruding visitors.

"It's fucking freezing. What are you guys doing out here?" I shoved my hands into my pockets.

"Just keeping an eye on things. Shelton insisted we do a little stake out to make sure nothing unexpected happens." Nate's grin grated on my nerves. "You shouldn't have a problem sleeping. We'll be out here all night."

Wonderful. In other words…Alex and I weren't going anywhere. Not until after I kept my word and fought in this damn match. A door creaked open behind me, and I heard the duffle thump onto the seat. The door shut with a bang that echoed through the night, and Alex returned to my side, her strength quiet but steady. She laced her fingers with mine, and that same uneasy feeling I'd had during my meeting with Shelton in the barn came over me again. Probability was high that he'd try to stop us from leaving at all.

22. END GAME

ALEX

Instead of a text with the location and time, Rafe received two gun-toting escorts the following night. They drove us to wherever the fight was being held, remaining frustratingly silent, and the situation was too similar to finding ourselves locked in the back of a trunk together. The way Rafe held onto my hand hinted that maybe he felt the same way.

Follow my lead. I'll get you out of this, I promise.

Rafe's words—whispered to me as we slid from the back of their souped-up SUV—bounced around my head as we entered a dilapidated warehouse. The furious vibe within these slab walls hit me instantly. The place was packed with people, the crowd consisting mostly of men.

As our henchmen escorts weaved a path for us, every man in a ten-foot vicinity attached his lust-filled gaze to my ass, though most were too busy taking a drag off a cigarette or swigging from a bottle of beer to say anything.

I clenched my fists to keep from tugging my black skirt down my thighs, past the lace tops of the stockings I wore. Men lost their minds when confronted with lace and a garter belt. I hadn't wanted to dress provocative, but Rafe said Shelton demanded it.

Rafe flung an arm over my shoulders and tucked me into his side. His hold was possessive, but also protective, and he glowered at anyone brave enough to look at me.

There were a lot of brave men here.

The man I'd spied talking to Rafe in the barn a few days ago headed us off with a low whistle.

"I'm Shelton," he said, taking my hand and brushing his wide mouth over the back. I yanked my hand from his.

Seemingly amused by my objection to being touched, he turned to Rafe with a small smile. "Your girl is a looker. I can see why you tried to run."

"Like I told your goons," Rafe said, sneering at the two men we'd followed inside, "I was just putting some shit in my truck."

Shelton waved his words away. "You're here, so consider us square." He leaned in close to Rafe. "We'll be *real* square after you make me a load of cash tonight."

"We're gonna have problems if you don't get the fuck out of my face."

"Whoa," Shelton said, stepping back. "What's with the hostility?"

"You tell me. You're the one siccing your dogs on me."

The other men bristled, but Shelton held up a hand. "Everybody relax. Nate and…" His eyes narrowed at the bigger of the two. "What the fuck is your name again?"

"Larson, sir."

"Drop the sir." Shelton pointed behind him, toward a door beyond a stack of crates. "Go make sure De Luca junior's nice and comfy. Keep him contained until the fight starts."

The other two men scuttled off. The way Shelton's predatory gaze bounced between Rafe and me was unsettling. I didn't like him. I didn't like this place. Most of all, I didn't like the thought of Rafe fighting my brother.

"You're not going to be happy about this, Mason, but I need you to do something for me."

"Why ask then?" Rafe said, and I winced at his tone. He wasn't playing nice at all. Not that I blamed him. But why piss off this guy unless we had a reason to? He said we were taking off as soon as the fight was over…unless he didn't think that was going to happen.

"Normally, I wouldn't, but I don't see a way around it. You want De Luca, and I want him in that cage with you." Shelton scratched his nose for a second. "Problem is, he's not budging unless he talks to your girl first."

Rafe tensed beside me, his body ready to burst into action. I couldn't see the adrenaline storming him, but I sensed it like an intangible wave in the air.

"I'm sure your guys can convince him."

"That isn't how I operate. He'll fight because he wants to fight." He gestured at me. "And if he doesn't talk to her first, he ain't cooperating."

"You mean we have a choice?" Rafe let out a bitter laugh. "So you won't mind if Alex and I take off then."

"Zach's a little tied up right now, but you're standing here free as a bird. Don't push me, Mason. Let him have five minutes with your girl. My guys will make sure he doesn't lay a finger on her."

Rafe was about to put up the fight from hell, I could already tell, but I stepped out of his grasp. "I'll do it."

"No!" Rafe's voice thundered through the warehouse, and the raucous chatter fell silent.

Ignoring him, I kept my gaze on Shelton. "I'll talk to him, but just the two of us."

Rafe wrenched me by the arm until we were eye to eye. "This isn't happening."

I glared at him. This was my chance to try and talk some sense into Zach. If I could get my brother to back down, maybe this match wouldn't end in death.

"This isn't up to you," I said. "He's running things." I threw Shelton a challenging look. "Aren't you?"

"You got that right."

"Take me to him then," I said, stepping to Shelton's side before Rafe could stop me.

"I'm gonna blister your ass for this," Rafe warned.

God, I hoped so, because that would mean he was still alive to do so. The air between Rafe and me grew thick with anger and sexual tension, but it dissipated when Shelton grabbed my arm and hauled me toward the door at the back of the building.

"Go warm up," he barked at Rafe. "She'll be fine."

Rafe wasn't listening. His furious footfalls pounded behind us, and the only thing keeping him outside that room was Shelton and his men.

"I swear to God, Alex—" The door slammed shut, silencing Rafe's threats of retribution.

Disquiet settled on the room like a blanket. Zach sat in a chair with his hands tied at his back and his feet secured to the legs. Letting out a breath, I took a cautious step forward, satisfied that he couldn't corner me. I was safe, no matter how fast my heart raced. He *couldn't* touch me.

"You look good, Lex." His hazel eyes lowered to my thighs, zeroing in on the tops of my stockings. "I'm surprised he let you in here," he said.

I jerked a thumb behind me. "If you couldn't tell, he wasn't happy about it. He didn't have much choice though."

Zach nodded. "These guys can be very persuasive."

"It was my decision."

He sat up a little straighter. "What?"

"I wanted to see you." I leaned against the cold, gritty wall and tried not to wring my hands.

"Why?" His voice cracked, and he stared at his feet for a few seconds. Was he feeling *guilty*? No way in hell. I couldn't believe it.

"He's going to kill you, Zach."

"You're worried about me?" He lifted a surprised brow.

"I'm worried about *him*." I stomped across the floor and halted a foot in front of Zach. If they hadn't tied him to that chair, he could have touched me. He *would* have touched me. "Don't force his hand. Please. If you ever cared about me at all, then don't take him from me."

He probably thought I meant in the physical sense, but deep down I knew what little sanity Rafe held onto would shatter if he went through with this. All the shit he'd gone through, especially these past few months, had taken a toll on him. I recognized someone on the brink because I'd been there.

Zach let out a bitter laugh. "You think I can take Rafe, do you? Is that what you're worried about?" He gave a pointed glance at his tied-up state. "Do I look capable of going against Shelton's underground champ?"

"That's not what I meant." Of course, I knew Zach was a threat, but I didn't believe Rafe would let him get the best of him. Not again. I believed him when he said he would come away from this fight the winner, if for no other reason than to keep me safe. But the what-ifs strangled me.

"Rafe's been through hell and back. If tonight ends in —"

"I've been to hell and back," Zach shouted, and to my utter shock, he squeezed his eyes shut to hide the tears threatening to spill over. "Lex, my hell started the day I saw Dad drive my mom away with his fucking fists. It started the day I saw you as more than my sister. It started the day you saw Rafe fucking Mason as more than my best friend."

Stumbling backward, I gulped. "It's not too late to do the right thing." But I realized something then— something that twisted everything around until the lines not only blurred, but they bent and broke. I needed Rafe the way Zach had always needed me. What an intricate web we weaved.

"That's not even the worst of it, Lex. Dad's the reason your mom is dead."

A loud fist pounded on the door, and I jumped. "We're not done in here!" I strode to the door and turned the lock on the handle. "If you come in here, he's not fighting," I shouted through the barrier keeping them out of this room.

Commotion sounded on the other side, and the knob clicked back and forth. Voices escalated, Rafe's especially, demanding that someone knock the door down.

I whirled on Zach, my hands fisted at my sides. "What are you talking about?"

"I wanted to tell you so many times..." He sniffled, blinked, and a wave of tears trailed down his scruffy cheeks. "She didn't kill herself, Lex. Yeah, she saw us that night, but she was gonna do the right thing. She was planning to leave my dad and turn me in. She fucking loved you." He jerked his head back and forth. "She would've done anything for you."

Something cold fisted my heart. "Why?"

"Dad wasn't about to let her destroy our lives. I'm telling you, Lex, he killed her and made it look like a suicide."

"No." I gaped at Zach, my mind spinning, trying to make sense of this abstract canvas he painted. The torn masterpiece of hidden truths, rough around the edges with harsh clarity. I knew him well—too well. Better than any sister should know a brother, and I knew he was speaking the truth.

But I couldn't fall apart now. I had to hold it together long enough to get through this night. And that made me angry.

"Why are you telling me this now?"

"I'm not making it out of here." The hazel in his eyes sharpened like always when he was passionate about something, usually me. "No matter what happens, stay away from Dad."

My jaw unhinged. I was speechless.

"I want you more than I've ever wanted anything," he said, "but you want him. And I'm not stupid. He wants me dead."

"He was your best friend! You don't have a clue what our lie started all those years ago. People have *died* because of it. Rafe's not the same guy you knew before we sent him to prison."

"I only know one thing for certain. Shelton got me out of that Mexican prison. He brought me here so Rafe could kill me inside that cage. The guy hates Dad's guts."

"I don't believe you."

"It's true. I overheard his guys talking. This is about revenge, and we're all playing into his hands."

"I heard what you told Rafe in that barn. You weren't shy about your hatred."

"What else was I supposed to say? I hate his guts, Lex. He took away the only thing I care about in this world."

"I'm not a thing."

"You know what I mean."

191

"No. I think you said exactly what you mean. You've always seen me as a thing, a piece of property."

He hung his head. "Then let's get this over with. Let him have his shot at me."

Panic seized me. I didn't know for certain that Rafe would kill him, and I had a hunch that Zach was feeding me a line of bullshit, preying on my vulnerability. He'd always been a master at manipulating me. Even so, I didn't want Rafe to go down this road. Not if I could stop it. I'd witnessed how getting his hands dirty had affected him—it was the reason he'd bolted six months ago.

And as much as I hated to admit it, even to myself, I didn't want to see Zach dead either.

Another fist rattled the door. "He's got ten minutes, then the boss wants him in that cage. Make it happen."

"I'm working on it!" Footsteps faded, and my gaze darted between the only window in the room and Zach's bound form slumped in the chair. I deliberated for a few seconds, my gaze swerving back and forth, indecision warring in my heart. As I hurried across the room and began working on the knots in the rope, a voice within screeched its objection.

What the hell was I doing?

Saving Rafe.

"What are you doing, Lex?"

I shot Zach a startled look. He'd grabbed the question

from my mind and had spoken it aloud.

"Something undeniably stupid." I released one leg then went to work on the other. "You can get out through that window over there," I said, pointing toward the rectangle pane of glass I prayed wasn't sealed shut. "I'll tell them you need a few minutes. I'll lock the door to give you time, so don't get caught."

"Why are you helping me?" I moved to his back and slowly worked the knots loose that trapped his wrists.

"I'm helping him."

As soon as the rope fell to the floor, he sprang to his feet, rounded the chair before I could blink, and pulled me against his chest. In the space of five seconds, I realized I'd made a dire mistake, and I almost screamed for help, but his mouth crashed onto mine and muffled my protests. His arms held me in a vise, and he bit down on my tongue just enough to knock the fight from me.

And then he let me go with a tortured sigh.

I shoved him until he crashed into a table. "Don't you fucking touch me," I said, my words a whisper of fury. I jabbed a finger in the direction of the window. "Get the fuck out of here, Zach. I swear on Rafe's life, if you ever come back I'll kill you myself." I retreated, heading to the door, my heart knocking around in my chest.

With a quick upward lift, he opened the window and let in the frigid winter air. He poked his head out, glanced downward, then pivoted to face me. "You've changed," he said, his tone holding a note of surprise.

"You mean I'm not the same spineless victim you screwed for years? Not bendable anymore?"

He gnawed on his lip. "I'm sure you're bending plenty. Just not for me."

"Better go," I said, refusing to go into my relationship with Rafe.

He hoisted himself through the opening, dropped to the other side, and popped his head up to give me one last look. "Tell him I said hi."

And then he was gone.

23. FORFEIT

RAFE

"Calm down. It's only been fifteen minutes. They're family," Shelton said with a shrug. "I'm sure they've got some catching up to do."

Rather than justify that asinine comment with a response, I continued my pacing outside the cage. Shelton's goons wouldn't let me near that fucking door because they knew I'd bust my way through it.

But fuck if I didn't take my eyes off it.

When it finally opened, and she stepped out, I was crawling out of my skin. I shoved two guys out of my way and went straight to her. "I'm so fucking pissed at you right now."

"I'm fine." She pointed at the door. "He said he'll

fight, but he needs a few minutes." She wouldn't meet my eyes, and that was the first clue something was wrong. The second was when Shelton tried the door and found it locked.

"Someone get me a key *yesterday*!"

Alex whirled, her eyes wide. "I must've locked it on my way out."

I grabbed her shoulders, alarmed by her rattled tone. "Did he hurt you?"

She shook her head. "He told me some upsetting things. I'll tell you later."

Shelton stomped toward us. "While they're taking care of this snafu, let's get the show started. People are getting antsy." He waved a hand in Alex's direction. "Strip her and chain her up over there," he ordered, pointing to a set of chains dangling a few feet from the cage.

"Excuse me?" I asked with a dangerous edge.

"You ain't deaf. I said strip her. I want her on display."

The dark cloud that passed over Alex's face alarmed even me. She wrestled from my grasp and popped the buttons on her top before sliding the shirt down her shoulders, then she unzipped the skirt and let it pool around her feet.

"Is this good enough?" she asked Shelton. "Or do you expect me to get naked for your perverted friends?"

"It's just business, honey." Shelton's mouth twitched into a grin. "She's got spirit. I like her." He walked away, muttering how this night was going to be a lesson in entertainment.

I trapped her arm in a painful grip and hauled her toward those fucking chains. "That was stupid."

"I'm a human being, not an object. If he wants my skin on display, I can do it myself."

"I meant going in to see Zach."

We stepped onto a platform a few feet from the cage, and I positioned her underneath the chains. Her gaze settled on that damn door Zach hid behind. He must have known how this was going to end. With quick, jerky motions, I buckled her wrists into the cuffs and stretched her arms above her head.

My mouth was a hard line, my touch rough and unforgiving, but when our eyes met and held, the angry beast inside me went into hibernation. She had me so fucking whipped. I slid my palms along her arms and brushed the sides of her heaving tits. Her matching black and red bra and panties were made of lace, barely there— meant to entice and seduce. Those scraps of fabric did a hell of a job tantalizing me, but I hated how every other fucker in here saw what I saw.

It wasn't supposed to be like this.

I leaned close enough to taste her lips, and the steady racket of voices receded. Only Alex and I existed in that moment, standing on the precipice of simmering hell. I think we both knew it was coming. Unable to resist, I pressed my mouth to hers and breathed her in.

"Before you know it, we'll be in my truck driving to God knows where. Maybe we won't fucking stop, but at least it'll be you and me together." I inched back and stared into her eyes. "I meant what I said at your house."

"What was that?"

"About marrying you. Eventually, we'll make it there. We'll find a space that's ours where the only struggle we'll face is keeping our hands off each other." I couldn't help but smile. "Though I think that's a fight we'll never win."

Her worried eyes veered to that locked door again. "I don't wanna lose you," she whispered. "Zach can torture me every day for the rest of my life, and it won't break me like losing you will."

"I'm not going anywhere. Everything's gonna be okay. Do you trust me?"

"Of course I do, but…" She drew in a jittery breath.

"What is it?"

"Please don't hate me."

A heavy sense of dread took root in my stomach. "What happened in there?"

"Something you're not going to like." She lifted her head just as Shelton and Nate approached the door, keys jingling. "Get me out of these cuffs!" she said with an alarming note of urgency.

Fuck. This did *not* sound good.

As they went through the various keys on that ring, I

unbuckled Alex's wrists, and we stepped down from the platform. They kicked the door wide open, and obscenities filled the air. I pushed Alex behind me as they marched in our direction.

"Where is he?" Shelton demanded, his mouth a thin, dangerous line. This was the most pissed off I'd seen him.

Acting fast, and on pure instinct, I grabbed Alex, one hand clamped around her chin, the other gouging her shoulder, and forced her to her knees. My hand slid from her chin and wrapped around her neck. "What the fuck did you do?"

The crowd spoke in hushed, excited whispers. Maybe, just fucking maybe, if I could give them a show and convince Shelton I'd had nothing to do with Zach's disappearance—which was too fucking true to be funny —we could get out of here in one piece.

"I asked you a question!"

"I let him go!" she said.

Shelton punched a crate, and everyone within ten feet of him jumped. Including me.

"Find him. *Now!*" he ordered his guys, voice an echoing thunder through the warehouse. He glowered at Alex, his stature towering over her. Every muscle in my body was poised to protect her from him, but I held my ground, straddling the line between furious boyfriend and loyal fighter who was on *his* side in this.

I lugged her to her feet by the hair, eliciting a sharp cry of pain. "I'll deal with her," I told Shelton. "Just find that fucking bastard, and tell me the instant you do."

Shelton took a deep breath and nodded. I led Alex to a corner of the room that wasn't as crowded and forced her ass into a chair. Fingers curling around the hem of my sweatshirt, I yanked it up my torso and over my head, then tossed it to her.

"Why'd you do it?"

She pushed her arms through the sleeves before tugging the material over her face. "I couldn't watch you kill him."

"You still have feelings for him." I bunched my hands and barely kept myself from trying to plow through the wall of cement at her back. Probably not the best outlet for my rage.

"Not in the way you're thinking. He's my brother, Rafe, or at least he was…at some point."

"He's the fucker who *raped* you," I growled.

"I know!" She jumped to her feet and met me head on. "And you're the fucker I'm in love with. You're the fucker who's not gonna kill *ever* again." She grabbed my face, her fingers tight around my jaw. If the wild look in her eyes hadn't entranced me—if we weren't surrounded by a bunch of people—I would have stripped her scant panties from her ass and fucked it.

Hard.

Until she cried from the pain then begged to come.

As it was, I stood my ground and let her have this moment.

"You promised we were getting out of this, Rafe. So do it. Keep your promise this time. Zach is gone. He's not coming back."

"How can you be so sure about that?"

"Because I swore on your life I'd kill him myself if he did. He's *not* coming back."

Her words fucking pummeled me. She'd do anything for me. That much was true. If she'd used my life as a device to swear on, then she was dead serious. "God, I fucking love you right now."

She furrowed her adorable brows. "Because I let him go?"

"Because you're willing to kill him yourself if he comes back."

Shelton and Nate approached, and Alex and I cooled the frantic fuck-each-other vibes traveling between us.

"Did you find him?" I asked.

"'Fraid not," Shelton said. "I know you wanted a shot at him." He sent a nasty glare toward Alex. "Get your woman in line, Mason. I'll call you when I find him. This ain't over."

"Fuck no, it's not. I told you I can't risk him on the loose."

He turned toward the people still waiting for a fight.

"Listen up, everyone!" His voice bellowed through the warehouse. "We got a little situation, so we'll have to do this another night." A collective groan traveled through the room. Shelton raised his hands. "Hey, all bets stand. The fight will happen. I'll send texts out when it's time."

As the crowd grudgingly began to disperse, Shelton slapped me on the back. "Nate and…what's-his-name will drive you back to the boat. They won't be happy to deal with the shitty weather for another day or so, but I won't let you be sitting ducks. Until we find Zach, you'll have protection 24/7."

He meant *we'll be watching you 24/7*. I was unarmed since Shelton had confiscated my gun while Alex was inside that damn room with Zach. How the fuck were we going to get out of here?

24. BREAKING FREE

RAFE

The stubborn silence between us unsettled me. Everything about this night unsettled the fuck out of me. Alex perched on the couch, her shoulders slumped, eyes downcast. I stood in front of her and propped my back against the side of the bench. It took everything in my power to keep my hands off of her. If I touched her now, I might lose control and do something I'd regret.

"I'm so fucking furious with you right now."

"I know," she said, picking at her cuticles. I gnashed my teeth. If she went for her skin, that would be it. I'd make her hurt in a bad way…in the same fucking way her actions tore me to shreds.

What she'd done felt a lot like betrayal, though I knew

she hadn't meant to betray me. She'd thought she was doing the right thing by letting that piece of shit go. Nothing in my standard arsenal of punishment would fix this.

I crossed my arms, trying to contain the energy flowing through me. "What were you thinking?"

She shook her head. "I don't know."

I let out a sigh and settled next to her on the couch. Resting my elbows on my knees, I dragged both hands through my hair. We had bigger problems to deal with, but at the moment, all I could think about was what had gone on in that room. Had he touched her?

"What did he say to you?"

"He said my dad killed my mom."

I lifted my head and gaped at her. "I did not just hear that right."

"You heard right." Her monotone voice dug underneath my tight grasp on control. Not only did I want to take a belt to her ass to work off this anger, but I wanted to demolish that listless void in her.

I wanted to kill Zach more than ever because he'd done this to her. Again. The fucker had played with her emotions.

"And you believe him?"

"I guess so." She shrugged. "Maybe. He could've been feeding me a line. But I know him, Rafe." With a hard swallow, she peeked at me from beneath her lashes.

"He also said Shelton was behind his escape. He orchestrated the fight as revenge. Guess you're not the only one who wants Zach dead."

A persistent throb started in my temples. I rose to my feet, propping both arms on the opposite wall. Giving her my back. "Guess you're the only one who wants him alive."

"That's not why I did it!" The boat swayed with her movement. She gripped my shoulder and yanked until I turned around. "What happened to loving me, huh? Deep down you knew that fight was a no-win situation."

"That fight is still happening, sweetheart. We're stuck, so unless you have an idea on how to get past the goons with the guns out there," I said, words blasting through the dim space like a vicious bullet, "I'm out of ideas." I swung my arms outward. "We could've been on our way outta here, but you had to let him go."

"How do you know Shelton is gonna let you walk away from this?" She jabbed a finger into my chest. "You're too valuable. I don't know much about this world of yours, but I know that much."

"Then you know that getting out of here is gonna be dangerous."

"We made it out of that tunnel," she pointed out.

"Barely. We got lucky."

A shrill ring sounded, accompanying the vibration in my pocket. I welcomed the intrusion because we were going in circles. I strode into the galley, needing to put some distance between us, and barked a hello.

"Why the fuck is Nate camped outside your boat?" Jax's voice sounded strained as if he'd inhaled a drag of nicotine before speaking. The subsequent exhale hinted that I was spot on.

"Thought you'd be in Mexico by now."

"I was headed that way."

"What happened?"

"Couldn't leave things like this. So how'd it go?"

I glanced over my shoulder and caught Alex digging into her left wrist. I snapped my fingers to get her attention. Her startled eyes veered my way, and I gave her a look. The look.

Stop fucking hurting yourself.

She let go of her wrist, and I leaned against the sink, keeping my focus on her. "It didn't go," I told Jax. "My stubborn, headstrong little vixen agreed to meet with the bastard. And get this—you're gonna love this—she helped him *escape.*"

"Well," he said, barely containing a snort.

"Sound fucking familiar?"

"Hey man, I'm with her on this. You went off the rails, and she wasn't even around to see how bad it got."

"Part of that was your fault."

"Why do you think I'm so fucked up over this?" Jax practically shouted, so loud even Alex heard him. "That's why I'm back, even though I should be all over this lead. I'm here to make sure you get the fuck out of there."

"We tried taking off right after you called. Nate and his buddy stopped us, and Shelton took my gun tonight too."

"What about the piece you lifted from Alex's house the night you grabbed her?"

"I got rid of it, so until an opportunity opens, we're stuck."

"You're still hoping to finish what you started. That's what you're really saying, right?" Jax sighed. "Let me guess. Shelton's looking for Zach as we speak."

"Something like that."

"You stubborn fool." The click of a lighter sounded. Jax only chain-smoked when he was stressed. "I'll take care of the idiots in the Escalade. Give me fifteen. I'll call you." The line went dead.

"Fuck." I jammed my cell into the pocket of my jeans. He was getting into the habit of hanging up on me, and I didn't like it.

"What's going on?" Alex asked.

"Jax is up to something. He said to be ready in fifteen."

She stood and glanced down at the sweatshirt that nearly swallowed her whole.

"Get dressed," I said. "Wear something warm with layers." For all I knew, the bag in my truck had grown legs and walked off. Hopefully, no one had messed with it, but we might be stuck with nothing more than the clothes on our backs, at least for a few days.

While Alex disappeared into the bedroom to dress, I pulled out our coats and flung them onto the sofa, then raided the drawers in the galley in search of a pocketknife.

Fuck, I'd miss this boat. The first day I set foot in the area, I happened to stumble upon a guy wanting to sell it. I'd had the cash, and something about the craft called to me. Maybe the idea of living on water was just…familiar. The only comforting thing I'd allowed myself to cling to back then. But it was time to lay that part of my life to rest. The boat would become an abandoned casualty of circumstance.

Alex returned fully dressed in jeans, a long-sleeved shirt, and a sweater. "What about your son?" she asked, tossing my sweatshirt to me. "Will leaving like this put him in danger?"

"No." I pulled the shirt over my head and picked up our coats. "I haven't told anyone about him. Only you and Jax know."

She settled onto the bench, her expression anxious, and tapped the tabletop with her nails.

Now all we had to do was wait. I peeked between the curtains but couldn't see shit through the fog. What the fuck was Jax up to? A few more minutes passed, and I began pacing. No way in hell could I sit still like Alex.

We both jumped when my cell let out another shrill ring. I dug the damn thing out, almost dropping it, and asked Jax what the hell was going on.

"Take Alex and go!" he shouted. "Don't stop for anything. I mean it. Get in your truck and get the fuck outta here."

"What did you do?"

"I took a page from Cleft's book. Now get moving. I'll call you soon," he said, and then the fucker hung up on me again.

"Let's go." I grabbed Alex's hand and practically dragged her to the staircase. The instant we reached the deck, smoke drifted to my nose, but it didn't hold the same scent like smoke from a fireplace or a wood stove. Through the fog, I spied an eerie orange glow in the distance, in the vicinity of the barn where I'd pounded out my helplessness, rage, sorrow, and every other emotion known to man for the past six months.

"Is that a…?" Alex squinted through the orange haze.

"A fire? I think so. C'mon." I moved toward the dock, but Alex halted, a natural reaction for her when water was involved. Instead of trying to talk her through her fear, I hoisted her over my shoulder and carried her, lifting one leg then the other onto the dock. Voices drifted to us from afar. Sirens would sound any minute. Nate's SUV was abandoned, doors left open.

Reaching my truck, which stuck out like a sore thumb

despite the fog, seemed to take forever. Each second presented a threat.

Someone would stop us.

Shoot us.

Kidnap us.

Aliens would fucking land because getting behind that wheel and leaving this place a distant memory seemed impossible. Alex must have felt the same way. Her fingers dug into my back a little deeper with each step. I opened the passenger door, shoved the duffle bag over, and set her on the seat.

"Is this really happening?" she asked as I tightened the belt snug across her lap and chest.

"This is really happening." I slammed the door, hopped into the driver's side, and sped the fuck out of there.

25. BORN AGAIN

ALEX

Six months later

"Come in the water, Alex." He applied a gentle pull on the chain linked to the collar entrapping my neck.

I cowered at the edge as water lapped my toes, buck-naked. The sun blared heat through the trees, and though Rafe said the water wasn't icy cold, I wasn't so sure about that.

Of course, that wasn't the reason I didn't want to go in.

"Don't make me do this," I pleaded. And make me, he would, unless I was able to convince him not to drag me in by that chain. My hands were cuffed behind me, leaving me helpless to his will.

"You're coming in this water. Question is, do you want in the easy way, or the hard way?"

"No way," I said, then bit my lip.

"Sweetheart," he said with another tug on the chain. I braced my heels on the ground. "You've gotta conquer this fear. One of these days, we're gonna go back to the island. I want you free of fear. I want you to fucking trust me."

A sob tried bursting free, but I held it in and took a tentative step forward, sinking my toes in. The floor of the lake was sandy, soft, and it settled under my weight.

"Good girl."

I'd barely taken a step, but his approval warmed me more than the sun ever could. Another step brought me fully into the water, just up to my ankles. Rafe stood hip deep several yards in front of me.

"Keep walking towards me, babe. I promise, when you get here, I'll make it worth your while."

A delicious shiver trailed down my legs. I took another step, then another, certain my heart would burst from my chest. I glued my gaze to him, afraid to look anywhere else.

His eyes roamed over my puckered nipples, and he licked his lips. "You're doing great."

"I really hate you right now."

"Get your ass over here, and I can guarantee I'll have

you declaring your love for me to God and anyone else in earshot."

No one else was out here, which was the point. We'd found a place so secluded to set up camp, I wasn't sure even Bigfoot could find this place. I spanned the last few feet and stood before him, collared, my hands useless, and waist deep in water.

This was a test of trust, in addition to pushing me beyond my phobia. He unhooked the chain from my throat and tossed it to shore, then he cupped his hands in the water and released it over my breasts. The cool drops dribbled over my nipples, and I whimpered.

Giving me a lopsided grin, he brushed his thumb over one aching bud before sliding his palm down my stomach. His fingers slid between my thighs, circling my clit.

"Oh God…Rafe…"

He hoisted me in his arms, pulling my chest flush with his, and stepped backward.

"Rafe?" I shrieked.

Deeper. He was taking us deeper.

His mouth claimed mine, hushing my objections. At some point I stopped fighting altogether, too caught up in the skill he used in fucking my mouth with his wicked tongue. We kissed for years in those few seconds, until we parted in the midst of heavy breathing that seemed so loud, it was difficult not to imagine our desire echoing off the mountains.

"Are you scared now?"

"No," I said, only now realizing how the lake rose to my shoulders. One slight dip, and we'd go under.

But he held me tight in his embrace, effectively trapping me without the use of even my arms, and I'd never felt safer or more treasured. I gazed at him in awe, in wonder, certain I'd burst with this feeling...whatever *this* feeling was.

Love was too weak a word and did nothing to encapsulate the degrees of our bond. I loved him, I did, but I needed him. The stark realization made my blood sizzle. As crazy as it sounded, my life and my soul were connected to his.

"What's wrong?" he asked in a whisper that teased my lips.

I blinked several times, trying to hold back my tears even though I wasn't supposed to. These tears I didn't want to shed. They were drops of...God...drops of sick happiness because no one in their right mind should rejoice at experiencing such an all-consuming possession.

"Nothing," I said, blinking the salty drops down my cheeks for him to eat up. "Nothing at all. I'm just so fucking..."

"Happy?" The word rumbled from his mouth with a groan. Grabbing my ass in his strong, capable hands, he hiked me up, his arms straining with the incredible strength he exerted in keeping me from tipping backward. I wound my legs around his waist and gripped him with my thighs.

"Baby," he said, grunting as he plunged into me, "I'm gonna fuck some more happiness into every piece of you, right in this fucking water." He bit my lower lip, tugged on it, and let it go. "This water can't touch the bravery in you."

I could hardly believe I was in the lake with him, and I wasn't scared. He gripped my hips and pulled me onto his cock over and over again. Not scared at all.

Delirious. I was delirious as I tilted my head back, closed my eyes, and lost myself to his thrusting cock, to the sway of the water around our interlocked bodies, to him dragging his tongue down my throat. How we got to the shore with him on his back, his hands guiding me as I rode him, I didn't know. Floating in a headspace that transcended time, I gave myself over to it.

As his mouth sucked my nipple deep, he freed my hands, and I flopped onto his chest, boneless. We rolled, our skin caked in mud from the lake and the ground we fucked on. It was dirty, primal, and I never wanted it to end. Being with him hurt so good. We cried out in synchronized agony then clung to each other as our breathing slowed. He shifted, so I sprawled halfway on top of him, one filthy leg trapped between his.

"I'll never fucking get sick of this, babe."

"Mmm, me neither." Despite the hard ground. Despite the way my skin itched from dirt, rocks, and leaves. Even knowing I'd have to go back into the water to clean up didn't extinguish the fire burning in me.

"It's weird being back," he said, a trace of sadness sneaking into his tone.

We'd spent months hopping from place to place, meeting new people, experiencing new towns. Every so often, he'd pick up a fight here or there to work off some steam…in addition to what he worked off with me. We'd found our slice of heaven in the simple act of not belonging anywhere. We only belonged to each other.

Maybe someday we'd go back to living the way normal people lived, though our version of normal was pretty damn skewed. Rafe talked about the island frequently, and I knew his desire to return was strong. If either of us had a home, that piece of land was it.

"What did your brother say when you called him?" I asked, lifting my head to meet his eyes.

"He was pissed that I disappeared for a year, to say the least."

"What about the island?"

"He and Jax are taking care of it. Plans to rebuild are already in progress."

"Do they need you there for it?"

He didn't say anything for a moment. "I'm not ready to go back, babe." He rolled until he propped over me.

"I'm content just to stay here with you forever. Let's just…be."

"I'm good with that plan."

"How about a real test? You ready for that?" He gave me a grin that was so full of mischief it made my spine stiffen.

I pointed at the lake. "*That* was the real test, Rafe. No doubt about it."

His gaze traveled up and down my body, roving over the dirt on my skin. "But now we're filthy."

"We've always been *filthy*."

"Don't I know it." He tweaked my nipple into an aching pebble, renewing the warmth between my thighs. Without warning, he jumped to his feet, and as he hauled me into his arms, I let out a startled cry.

A terrified cry.

"No!" I told him, pounding his chest as he cradled me against him.

He marched toward the water, the heated glint in his eyes already warming me up. Oh God. He was going to do it. We were going in over our heads.

"Hold on, babe. Close those gorgeous eyes and just let go." And with that, we took the plunge. Diving into darkness had never felt so good.

Acknowledgements

This series has been a crazy, rough ride, and I wouldn't have gotten through it without the support of you amazing readers. I owe you the biggest thank-you of all for diving into the darkness with me.

I also want to thank Deb and Rachel for offering their help as admins in the Naughty Nook group, to Momo, Deb, and Joanna for the fabulous music recommendations, to Kashunna and Momo for beta reading, and to the following blogs for basically being awesome: Confessions of a One-Click Addict/ Give Me Books, Rough Draft Book Blog, Books Over Boys, Bound By Books…I know I'm going to forget someone, so I'll just stop here. Truly though, I'm in awe at the number of bloggers that give their time freely in support of their favorite books. You guys are amazing.

Thanks to the following authors for wanting to party with me on Facebook: Pam Godwin, Clarissa Wild, Skye Warren, Carian Cole, Carmen Jenner, Chelle Bliss, Cassia Brightmore, M. Never, Harlow Grace, Shari Slade, Kitty Thomas, Kristin Elyon, and Amity Cross.

Deviant, book five in the Condemned series, is now available!

Sometimes light can be found in the dark. Rafe is a blazing sun in the center of my universe. He's my strength. The only man capable of healing me. He's the love of my life. He's also my enforcer. The strikes of his belt shield me from self-harm's temptation, but old habits are hard to break. No matter how much light we infuse into our deviant world, we still feed off each other's twisted desires.

Now I stand before him dressed in white, on the cusp of putting my fragile heart into his hands forever. But what if forever ends today? What if the past isn't finished with us yet? We've gone through hell to get here, and nothing and no one is going to take this away from us. Even if I have to kill for it.

Please visit my website to find where you can purchase Deviant:
www.authorgemmajames.com/books

About the Author

Gemma James is a USA Today and Amazon bestselling author of a blend of genres, from new adult suspense to dark erotic romance. She loves to explore the darker side of human nature in her fiction, and she's morbidly curious about anything dark and edgy, from deviant sex to serial killers. Readers have described her stories as being "not for the faint of heart."

She warns you to heed their words! Her playground isn't full of rainbows and kittens, though she likes both. She lives in Oregon with her husband and their four children—three rambunctious UFC/wrestling-loving boys and one girl who steals everyone's attention.

For more information on available titles, please visit www.authorgemmajames.com

Made in the USA
Lexington, KY
08 May 2019